# IDOLS
# OF
# ENDEAVOR

## BY
## MICHAEL J. ALSUP

Coastal Winds
Publishing House

Coastal Winds Publishing House
3167 63rd Street
Port Arthur, Texas 77640

For information contact: Coastal Winds Publishing House
Email: publisher@coastalwindspublishinghouse.co

ISBN: 978-1-7367302-0-1

Library of Congress Control No. 2021921876

_____

Publisher: Pamela Joy Licatino, Port Arthur, Texas

Author: Michael J. Alsup
Editor:  Pamela Joy Licatino
Cover design and layout: Pamela Joy Licatino
Printing/Distribution: Lightning Source /Ingram

# *DEDICATION*

To my loving wife, Lutz Alsup, who gives me moral support to continue writing my stories. For she understands what I must go through to bring this novel to life.

To my good friends Buddy and Nola Johnson. They have help me in so many ways of getting my story out to the world. Thanks for your kindness.

To my good friend Rev. Melvin Wiltz. He gave me the needed push to finish this story. For his kind words, I'm truly grateful.

To all of my Filipino friends. "Maraming Salamat."

"One day,
your
footprints
in the
sand
will have
many
followers."

# ~Chapter One~

Staring into empty space, I knew deep down in my soul that I must do something about these words that keeps scrambling around in my head. "There will come a time in your life that you must follow your heart."

Monday morning, I decided to call a Board of Director's meeting for ten o'clock. Standing in front of the Board of Directors who were chattering amongst themselves, I had a feeling no one was going to pay me any mind, even after I tried to get their attention, but to no avail. Picking up a pointing stick from the blackboard, I smacked the table so hard that it made a loud crackling sound and suddenly, the room went quiet!

"Now that I have everyone's attention, I have something important to say. AMN Industries, which I developed from the grassroots up, is doing very well in the business world. Four years after opening its doors, I have decided to step down as CEO to pursue my dream. "I'm leaving this company with the best people that any organization would be proud to have, and I would like Minda to take over my position as CEO."

Her smile was as big as I had ever seen. "Do you think?" was all she said.

I looked into her eyes. "I do."

At first, everyone groaned at hearing the news. The look on Neala's face told me that she was just knocked off her feet. I stayed quiet until the room went silent.

My father rose from his chair with a smile on his face. "I knew someday you would remove yourself from this company. I have always known you would follow your heart to pursue your dream."

"Minda, we welcome you with open arms." When everyone started clapping, Minda stood up and I could see tears in her eyes.

"I just want to thank all of you for giving me a chance."

My father responded. "We are not giving you a chance. You have proven yourself to all of us more than once. You've earned this right to move your life forward."

I stepped over to Minda and gave her a big hug. Whispering in her ear, "You take this company to the next level."

Neala looked at me with a raised eyebrow and great concern displayed on her face. "What's up?"

"I want to move forward in my life, that's all. I've decided to pursue my dream of teaching."

"Okay. Thanks for the heads up. I will need to find someone to relieve me from the security detail with this company."

"Oh no, I'm so sorry. I totally forgot about that. This idea just came to me this morning at breakfast. I know that if I don't push myself to the next level, I'll be moving backward instead of forwards."

Neala and I made our way to my office. "I need a plan."

Neala was sitting across the desk from me, rubbing her right temple for a brief moment. "Don't you have to be certified from the Department of Education in order to teach?"

"I do. Now let me think about this for a second." I went online to find the phone number of the Department of Education and placed a call. After their secretary answered, she put me through to a Mrs. Vega.

"I want to find out about what steps I must do in order to get a teaching degree."

Mrs. Vega went quiet for a little bit. "First things first. What is your name?"

"Oh! I'm sorry. My name is Ali Cruz."

"And how old are you?"

"I'm nine years old."

There was another pause on the line. Mrs. Vega's had this picture in her mind of a small child playing on the telephone. "I think you need to finish elementary school first, then high school and college. You cannot get a teaching degree without a college education."

I leaned back in my chair. It kind of made me laugh at her remark.

"Mrs. Vega, I have diplomas from all of these institutions. I just don't have a certificate saying that I can teach."

I think Mrs. Velga was hitting a boiling point. "There is only one person that I am familiar with that has done this. Though I have never met her, and her name escapes me right now."

"That person is me," I said.

With her voice up a couple of octaves. "Say what?" She stopped talking, and then asked, "Are you the young lady from the Albay Province?"

I raised my voice. "I'm the one. And I want to teach. But to do so, I need a certificate that says that I can."

Slightly embarrassed, she stated, "I'm so sorry. I thought you were a child trying to pull a fast one on me. In order to get you certified, you'll need to take a teacher's certification test. Let me see." I could hear her typing on the keyboard. "You can go to Zamora College in Bacacay and talk to the Dean. Her name is Mrs. Bautista. I'll send her a letter now telling her about you and what you're wanting to do. Oh Ali, if you ever want to teach here in Manila, any dean at any of our universities would love to have you on their teaching staff."

I had to fan my hand in front of my face. I know it doesn't

do much, but this conversation was getting a little warm.

"Thanks," I said, "for the offer, I'll consider it."

Hanging up the phone, Neala caught part of my conversation. "What did she have to say?"

"After I take the teacher's exam, I can teach anywhere I want to go."

Neala grinned. "I know that's right."

I placed a call to the Dean at Zamora College after a brief introduction. She then asked, "What day and time are good for you?"

"Today is Monday. I would like to do this tomorrow, if that's possible."

"That would be wonderful. It will give me time to prepare for the test that we give our students. Say nine a.m.?"

"I'm good with that," I said.

Neala waited for me to hang up. "I'll pick you up at eight-thirty."

Neala picked up her notes. "I need to take care of the security details for our company."

I headed to Minda's office. I saw her talking to a potential buyer of our product on the phone. As soon as she hung up, she smiled. "I'm going to like being the CEO of AMN Industries. I wish my parents could see me now."

"I think they are watching over you. You have made them so proud. I know I am."

*****

"I just got off the phone with the Dean of Zamora College. I'm going to take a test to see if I can teach here in the Philippines".

Minda wanted to make fun of me. "Do you have any wall space left at home or here for another diploma?"

"Not really. But hey, to do anything in this country or any

other place, you must deal with the government and all the red tape they can wrap you up in."

Minda laughed. "Tell me about it. Now, I have to deal with the mess that you gave me."

"Good luck with that," I said, giggling.

Minda gave me a high five.

Neala was sitting outside my house in her SUV at eight-thirty sharp. Getting in, I was buckling the seatbelt when I saw her smile. "You ready for this?"

"I sure am. It's time to start a new career."

Neala just shook her head. "Most kids your age would be worrying about taking an elementary school test. Here you are again taking another college exam."

"I know. It's kinda cool."

Walking into the main building, we headed straight towards the administration office. I could hear voices from the students in the hallway. *"What's a young kid doing here?"* Then a thought came to me. I might just be their teacher one day. That would give them something to talk about. I'm still not tall enough to reach the top of a blackboard.

A receptionist saw Neala and me walk into the office.

"May I help you?" she asked, looking at Neala.

Neala just pointed her finger at me. "She's the one who needs some assistance."

That answer threw her a curveball. She tried to clear her throat. "Aren't you a little young to be in college, young lady?"

Neala shook her head. "Another one." Then she shrugged her shoulders. "I guess it comes with the territory."

Looking up at Neala. "Yeah, I'm starting to get used to it." Changing subjects, "I'm here to see Mrs. Bautista. I have an appointment at nine a.m."

The receptionist went to her desk. "Your name?"

"Ali, Ali Cruz."

The receptionist was taken back a few steps. "Oh my. I was not aware of who you were. I'm so sorry."

"It's okay. I get this a lot."

Neala turned her eyes to the right side of her face. I could see an upwards grin.

Mrs. Bautista stepped out of her office with some documents in her hand. She stopped when she saw a childlike person talking with the receptionist.

"You must be Ali. I have a room set up for you to take your certification test. This test will take approximately two hours. Are you ready?"

'I am," I said.

"Good, then here are your papers. You may go into that room." I looked back at her. *'I've been here before when I took my test for a college bachelor's degree.'*

\*\*\*\*\*

In twenty-three minutes and twelve seconds, I opened the door. "Here's my test." The look I got from everyone in the administration office is something that I will never get over. Dean Bautista took my exam, and a student counselor went into the room I just left to grade it. Thirty-eight minutes later, they both stood in front of Neala and me.

Mrs. Bautista looked fluttered. "Ali, I have never met anyone who can do what you can do on a test in such a short amount of time. Have you ever had your IQ tested?"

"I have," I said.

"If you don't mind me asking, what did you score on it?"

"The machine can only go as high as three-hundred. The needle was pegged at that point."

"I don't think anyone in our country has ever accomplished this feat.'

"No one has that I'm aware of," I said.

"Oh, by the way. You've got a perfect score on your teaching exam. For the life of me, I cannot figure out how this is possible. The articles in Teachers Monthly Magazine mentioned you and your canny abilities to ace any test. Now, I got to see this very feat with my own eyes."

"Since I was given the gift of knowledge from our Lord Jesus Christ at the age of four, I've used my knowledge so far to start a new company here in Bacacay named AMN Industries. We have hired hundreds of Filipinos, and we are making our country safer from the typhoons."

Mrs. Bautista studied my face. "I've heard of it. I have a cousin who works there."

"Yesterday, I gave my CEO duties over to my dearest friend, Minda Torres. She received her college degree from the University of the Philippines at the age of nine. My youngest sister, Maria, is only five, and she is reading at the rate of a twelve-year old."

"But how is this possible. Are they related to you?"

"No, not at all. Minda use to live a couple houses down from me. Her parents were killed when a typhoon hit us a few years back. My parents also adopted Maria. My father was in Tacloban when they took a direct hit, and her parents were killed as well."

"So, let me get this straight, you've been teaching them?"

"I have," I said as I smiled.

"So, what are your plans?"

"I would like to find a place where I can teach students. I think I can help them become more intelligent. I would like to see the Philippines have some of the most brilliant minds in the world."

"That would be a monumental task, to say the least," Mrs. Bautista said.

"I know. And it's a challenge that I am willing to take."

I could see Neala smiling. "You should have seen the challenge Ali took on in Switzerland a few years back."

"What challenge was that?" Mrs. Bautista asked.

"I read every book the school had to offer besides the books given to the twenty-four students attending the school. I read all twenty-thousand of their books in the main library. This task took me about eight months to finish. The dean gave me a test on books chosen at random. Four other students wanted to take this test as well. One passed, but that was not the point. They took on something that they had never seen before. That is what I hope some students could do here."

"What school was that?" she asked.

"The World Study of Interacting Students. The only way a student can attend is by invitation from your government. I was there for eight months finishing up my challenge. Then I was asked to leave."

"Why would they ask you to leave?"

"Because they couldn't teach me anything that I didn't already know. All the teachers were going to quit if I didn't leave. So, I returned to the Philippines and started my own company. Now I'm here, and. I want to use the gift that God gave me to teach others."

"That's quite a remarkable story. You know that we are in March and our school year ends next month."

"I know. I would like to have a small room and a handful of students who wouldn't mind staying after class for a few hours until school ends. Then we can measure their progress to see if my teaching methods would benefit them."

"I like that idea," Mrs. Bautista said.

Grabbing her keys off of her desk. "Would you like to follow me?"

Neala and I walked beside her to a small room. It looked like it used to be a classroom with a chalkboard hanging on a wall.

"This used to be a small room for a lab. Now we use it for storage. You are welcome to use it if you want."

With a large smile. "I would like that very much."

"Now, as far as paying you a salary, we are not budgeted to add another teacher here at this time."

"That's okay. I'm being taken care of by my company."

"I'll make an announcement to see if any of our students would like to sit in on your class. When do you want to start?"

"Right now, if that's possible. All I need to do is start cleaning out this room."

"Oh my. Yes, of course," Mrs. Bautista said. "I'll have the custodian get on it right away." Removing a two-way radio, she summoned the custodian to the front storage room. Within ten minutes, a tall, lanky man walked up toward us.

"I'll need this room cleaned out as soon as possible. Take everything to storage room number three. And we'll need twelve desks brought in." The custodian got on his radio and called for several more hands to pitch in on the clean-out and bring the desks in.

While the room was being taken care of, Mrs. Bautista asked. "If you would like to go to lunch, the cafeteria is that way. When you get back, the room should be ready for you."

"Thanks," I said as Neala and I left. Standing in line, I noticed several students looking down at me. A girl of about eighteen years of age, with a smirk look on her face, asked me. "What are you doing here?"

I want to be polite to everyone, so I responded, "I'm going to start teaching here today." Several other students overheard our conversation. I watched a male student start mouthing off.

"You're not old enough to teach a dog a new trick." A thought came to mind, another Randy Johnson.

"Care to challenge me?" I asked.

"Yeah, sure. I challenge you to a math quiz."

"What are the stakes?" I asked.

"If I win, you leave this school to the adults and go back to elementary school." Several of his friends laughed and gave him a high-five.

I looked up at his stern face. "And if I win, you have to come to the class that I am teaching after school until the school year ends. Deal?"

"You got it," he said.

"Ok, meet me after class at the old storage room by the front office at four o'clock."

"Oh, by the way, whom am I talking to?"

"My name is Henry Mercado."

"Nice to meet you, Henry. My name is Ali Cruz."

Murmuring started to spread throughout the cafeteria. Some of Henry's friends patted him on his back. "You've just been had, my friend. She has an IQ that no one in our country, perhaps the world, has." Henry's eyes were opened wide. He gulped. "I didn't know," was all he said.

"Do you still want to challenge me?"

"I don't think I should. You know?"

"Yeah, I know, but never back away from your fear. To succeed in life, you must take on those fears and conquer them."

"Yeah, but I know that's a losing battle before it ever begins."

"Maybe so. But challenge yourself to take on something, even if it means defeat. You will never know what you are capable of until you try."

Henry smiled at me. "I like the way you think. Those are encouraging words to live by."

Word began to travel around the school like wildfire. Within an hour, every student knew of the challenge. Neala was sitting in the back of the room when Henry walked in with several of his friends.

I could see that he was shaking from just thinking about what he got himself into. Within the next two minutes, every chair was filled, and students were lining the walls inside my room and outside the doorway.

Mrs. Bautista heard all the commotion in the hallway.

"What's going on?" she asked.

"Henry Mercado challenged Ali Cruz to a math quiz."

"Thanks," she replied as she headed towards my little room.

Peering over the heads of several students in the doorway, I was giving a lecture about what was about to happen.

"I do not and will not ridicule any student. I am following my dream of teaching. I have asked Mrs. Bautista if I could teach here until the end of the school year. Most of you know that I just met Henry Mercado in the school's cafeteria not more than two hours ago. As soon as he heard who I was, he wanted to back down from our challenge. I asked him not to. Showing defeat before you ever start will not only make you weak, and not only in your own eyes, but to the rest of the world as well. You must take on your fears and try to conquer them. Never walk away. For they will eat you alive for the rest of your life."

Everybody clapped at the end of my lecture.

"Henry, are you ready?"

He gulped. "Yeah, I guess so."

Opening up his math book, he wrote a problem on the board. After he had finished, he stood back to look at his handy work. Several of the students wrote down what he had just written.

"May I?" He handed me the chalk.

I wrote the answer down in less than ten seconds.

A female student asked. "How do we know if your answer is correct?"

"That's a good question," I said.

"Would someone go and find a math teacher?"

Ten minutes later, a Mr. Ocampo entered my small room. He looked at the math problem on the board and the answer. "I was asked to come and look at a math problem?"

Mrs. Bautista was standing just inside the door. "Please check Ali's answer to the problem that Henry put onto the board."

Mr. Ocampo pulled out his scientific calculator from his pocket. Once the problem was entered, he looked at my answer.

"Her answer is correct." Pushing his wired-rimmed glasses back up, he looked at me. "I'm kinda curious. How long did it take you to answer the problem?"

Another male student who was leaning against the opposite wall said. "Ten seconds tops. And she did it without a calculator."

I stood next to Henry. "Do you want to continue?"

Henry smiled. "I need to try to answer your problem. I will never know unless I give it my best."

I was smiling back. "That's a good answer. If you want to stay after school for a couple of hours each day, I would like to work with you."

Henry looked at me. "I would like that."

I erased Henry's problem on the board. I thought about a good equation to use, then I wrote it on the board.

Walking away, I watched Henry study what I had written.

Henry smiled and asked. "May I?" As I handed him the chalk, he studied the problem and proceeded to put his answer down. The math teacher immediately saw what he had missed.

Walking back to the board. "Henry, you solved part of the problem." I pointed out where he was guided away from getting the correct answer. "The first part you answered correctly, but you forgot what this symbol means, and it caused you to miss the second part." I turned to the other students, "By the way, his problem was one of the issues that NASA had to solve on the ISS." The group of students was amazed.

"It is solving problems like this and many more that will

put you into the twenty-first century. There are thousands of companies all over the world who are looking for people who can solve problems and find solutions. As we move forward, the world will not sit back and wait for you to catch up. You must be on the cutting edge to take us into the next millennium. I'm looking for a small group of students who are willing to stay after school for a couple of hours and work with me." Out of the group who were in and out of the room, eight more, including Henry, wanted to try to advance.

"Would the students who said that they would stay, please don't leave just yet. I would like to talk to each of you." Everyone left except Mrs. Bautista, Neala, me, and the nine students.

As each student found a desk to sit in, Mrs. Bautista stood in front of the group. "If each of you will sign your name and your student number on this piece of paper, I will make a note into each of your files about how you want to advance to the next level. Since this is not a class that gives out grades, it will be noted."

"Will we be tested?" a male student asked.

"I will test you to see how well you are moving forward. The knowledge that you receive here will benefit you in your other classes. You could very well see your GPA go up."

Standing in front of each student, I asked. "What's your name? What grade level are you in right now? What is your major? And what are your plans when you graduate?"

"Now that I know a little about each of you, I will tell you about me. At the age of four, I passed every level of academics known. I met the President of the Philippines here and at his home. I was asked to attend a school in Switzerland called, *The World Study of Interacting Students*. I stayed for eight months and was asked to leave because the instructors couldn't teach me anything new, so I left and came back here. At the age of five, I started my own company, AMN Industries in Bacacay."

A young student asked. "Why would you give up a job that pays you very well?"

"Because I'm no different than you. I have a dream, and I must follow my heart until the end of my time on this earth. I want to teach students, such as yourself, to be the best that you can be. Maybe one day, you too will be able to help our fellow Filipinos and make their lives better. I hope each of you will follow your heart and pursue your dreams."

Henry stood up. "Because of you and your company, my family would not be here today. The shelter that was built in Tacloban, using your invention, saved them from despair. The old shelter was gone."

"Thank you, Henry. I want to help my country in anyway I can. I developed a product making cement stronger, and it has saved thousands of lives. I hope by teaching you and others like yourself that one day, you too can help the people in our country and the world."

"We'll start tomorrow. Hope to see everyone here."

Mrs. Bautista remained after the students left. "Your lecture should be given to the entire school. I even wanted to stay after class, just to hear you speak."

"Thank you," I said.

"Please stop by anytime and see how they are doing. Any feedback would be appreciated."

# ~Chapter Two~

With the thought of a satisfying day on my mind, I was glad to be home with my family. My mother looked up from doing her chores and cooking dinner. "How're things in your world?" she asked.

Setting down my briefcase, I gave her a hug. "It's good. I'll start teaching at Zamora tomorrow. My class starts at four p.m."

"Isn't that a little late to start a class?" she asked.

"It usually is, but the school year is over in a month. I wanted to get my feet wet and not wait to see if I could qualify to teach. I already have nine students who want to take my first class."

"That doesn't seem to be a lot of students who want a higher education."

"No, not at first. But I am hoping once the others find out that they can benefit from a different approach to teaching, they may want to join my class. My classroom is rather small. The dean put me in a storage room that used to be a lab from way back when, but not anymore"

"I see," my mother said.

Maria walked into the kitchen.

I knelt down to give her a hug as well. "How are you today?" I asked

"I'm good. Can you help me with my homework?"

"I sure can. Do you want to start now or wait until after we eat dinner?"

"Let's start now," she said.

"I like that." I spoke with so much excitement , "She's a go-getter, just like the rest of us."Minda appeared from our bedroom.

"Hey girl. How's the new job going?"

Minda ran a brush through her hair. "It's going okay. I've got a lot of things to learn, but I know it will come to me."

"I like the sound of that. You don't back down from a challenge." Minda smiled.

"You're the best teacher that anyone could ever have."

I think I blushed.

My mother interrupted. "Dinner is just about ready. Your father will be home soon. He's out running a couple of errands. You girls get washed up." The three of us responded. "Okay, Momma."

My father walked in as we were just sitting down at the dinner table. He set his things down so he could wash up to eat. He gave each of us a hug and kissed my mother. Minda looked at me nervously with her large eyes.

"What?" I said.

She just smiled. "The way my new parents are with each other reminded me of my own when they were alive." Once the dinner was ready and my mother sat with us, I said the blessing.

My father looked at me. "How did your test go, and did you get a job?"

I explained everything in detail. "Tomorrow will be my first day. My class does not start until four p.m. I'll be a little late getting home each night." My parents could hear the excitement in my voice.

My mother learned a long time ago not to judge me and my abilities. She made her thoughts known, "My daughter, at the age of nine, is teaching at a college."

I smiled at her. "I am, momma, and I'm looking forward to it."

As we sat there eating our dinner, a thought came to me, *'this is what parents are supposed to do with their children. Listen to them and guide them to make the right decisions in life. I know for a fact my parents did not expect that I would ever throw them a curveball and make adult decisions at my age. But they accepted the way that I am and are glad that I'm following my dream.'*

Our parents are the best thing that could have ever happened to us girls. To help others who have been left alone and in need of love and family. That was what our Lord had planned for us.

We were almost finished eating when my thoughts began to wander off. Both of my parents watched me. They could see that I had tears on my cheeks.

My mother became concerned about my sudden demeanor.

"Ali, are you okay?" she asked.

Wiping my face with my hand. "Yeah, I'm okay. Sometimes I think about how we all came together as a family and what it means to you two."

My two other sisters got up from the table and stood next to me. They too knew what I was talking about. Even my little sister Maria. We told her how she came to be with us. She never knew her parents. They were gone when she was just eight months old. My parents have always tried to instill in us that whatever happened in the past is gone forever, and nothing will ever change that. But we, as a family, can work for a better future for all of us. These words always comforted me, and I will teach them to my own family one day.

*****

Tuesday morning, Neala was sitting in front of my house at eight-thirty sharp. Seeing her from the front window, I walked out in my night clothes to talk to her.

"Come inside and have some coffee with me."

"That would be nice," she said.

Pouring her a cup, I watched her facial reactions. I could tell when something was bothering her.

"Let's sit. I can tell something is bothering you. Want to talk about it?"

Neala has always had the mindset of being upfront with me.

"I have heard on the street that a new synthetic drug will be on the market soon, but it has not yet been perfected. The side effects are horrendous or possible death. The word is that a drug lord is looking for a person who can perfect this stuff so he can sell it cheap on the streets. Does going down this road have a ring to it?"

I caught on to what she was saying. "It does."

Neala took a sip of her coffee. "This is just the beginning. There's no telling what will happen to you or your family. These crazy lunatics think that they can do whatever they want and to whomever."

Neala put her cup down. "I contacted the president to let him know what is going on in this province. He tells me that it's spreading across the nation at a rapid rate. He asked me to be extra vigilant with you."

"I see. So, I guess you and I will be spending a lot more time together."

Neala smiled. "We will."

I worked on putting a set of lesson plans together for my class while Neala did some checking around the property and out on the street. With nothing out of place inside or out, she headed back inside.

"Neala, I want to go to school a little bit earlier today. Since this is my actual first day, I want to make sure that everything is set up and okay."

"What time did you have in mind to leave?"

"We can leave around one-thirty or thereafter."

"That's fine," Neala said. Turning on the television, a special news alert came on. A tropical storm was developing out in the pacific. Reconnaissance aircraft were being sent to the area to investigate.

I sat down next to Neala. "I don't like to hear about these storms. They always cause major problems for everyone that's impacted."

Neala turned off the television.

"Want to leave now?" she asked.

I looked at the clock.

"Yeah, we can go. I don't like just sitting around here when I could be doing something useful."

Neala agreed. "I know what you mean."

As soon as we were in Neala's SUV and buckled in, she took notice of the traffic ahead of us. "Let's take the back road and see if we can bypass all of this mess."

Neala did a one-eighty in the middle of the road. Just as she straightened her SUV, she saw flashing red lights shining in her rear-view mirror.

Neala pulled over to the side of the road. Killing her engine, she waited for the officer to approach her side of the car. I caught sight of another officer coming towards my side view mirror.

"What's going on?" I asked.

"Not sure." Neala unholstered her gun and hid it from view. She rolled down the driver's side window, waiting to hear instructions from the officer approaching her. Holding out her Presidential ID so the officer could see that she was a government agent, he never looked at it.

He said, "Please step out of the vehicle." Exiting the car with her pistol stuck in her belt, the officer saw the gun and started to reach for his. Neala was on him in a matter of a second. The other officer took notice of what had just happened, so he removed his weapon and pointed it at me. Then, Neala removed the first officer's weapon from its holster. Pointing it at his head, she took control of the situation.

"Now tell me nice and slow why you stopped me. You can also tell your fellow officer to holster his weapon so he will not get hurt. I have no problem putting you two down. Do you understand?" His head shook. "Now tell him." Words were exchanged, but the other officer did not obey his command.

Neala responded. "You've got three seconds to live or die. Make your choice." He holstered his weapon. Neala held the first officer in a chokehold. He started coughing several times as Neala increased her grip.

"Now tell me just who are you, and what's your business with me?"

"With a raspy voice, we were told to stop an SUV matching yours. That you are with a drug lord that has moved into the area."

"Who gave you these orders?"

"Our captain."

Neala produced her identification again. "You see this? I'm with the secret service to our president. I have orders to protect that little girl by any means necessary. This may have been your lucky day. Tomorrow, your family would be putting flowers on your caskets. Now, call your captain." The officer made a radio call. After several minutes, a return call came through.

It seems this officer had gotten his information wrong, and this mistake nearly cost him his life and his fellow officer. He kept apologizing for being so stupid. Neala remained calm. After returning to her SUV, I was kind of excited to hear what all of this was about. As we drove off, I watched her eyes. I knew her brain was on high alert. She kept watching her mirrors. She saw the two officers talking to each other while getting into their patrol car. After putting several kilometers behind us, my curiosity got the better of me.

"Can you tell me what just happened and why I had a gun pointed at me?" Neala pulled over to the side of the road.

"Those two officers were told to stop us. Their captain gave them their orders. He thinks that we're drug dealers. I had to convince them otherwise, for this situation was not going to end well for either of them."

"Would you hurt them?"

"I will do whatever is necessary to protect you from any harm, even if it means taking another person's life. Do you understand?"

I sat very still for quite some time. Neala was not going to move until we had finished our conversation.

"This must be the beginning of the troubles that we discussed earlier," I said.

Neala looked directly towards me. "In this world that we live in, we must always be on alert to our surroundings at all times. Those two officers may not have received their orders from their captain, but from a drug lord who's looking for you and or your family."

"My family? What for?"

"To kidnap a member of your family to draw you into their trap. Once they get what they want, it usually doesn't end well for the people who were taken."

We pulled into the parking lot of Zamora College. Since I'm not considered faculty here, we had to park in the student area. Walking into the main building, students who were wandering the hallway, looked at me. I'm not sure if I will ever get used to not being starred at. Putting my key into the door lock, I saw Henry Mercado walking past me.

"Hello, Henry," I said in a joyful voice.

"Oh, hello, Ms. Cruz."

"Call me Ali," I said.

"Okay, Ali."

"Are you going to come to class today?"

"I'll be there. I'm looking forward to seeing what you can teach me."

"Great. See you then."

As soon as the four o'clock bell rang, students were scrambling in the hallways. I pulled out my seat chart to call each person by name. Nobody likes to be called "Hey you," or "What's your name again? It sounds very unprofessional."

As soon as everyone was seated, I noticed one chair didn't have a body in it. "Does anyone know," looking at my chart, "where Mr. Lobo is?" No one knew.

"Okay then, let's get started. I'm very fond of science and math. But I know twelve languages, history, politics, and any subject that you would like to cover."

Henry spoke up. "Science would be great. Most of us in here have the same science teacher."

"Okay. Since I don't have any of the books that you are using right now, may I borrow yours for a couple of minutes?"

Henry removed his book from his backpack. Walking over to my desk, he handed it to me.

"What chapter are you studying right now?"

"We are on chapter twelve." I opened his book and scanned every page in a matter of minutes. The class couldn't believe what I'd just done. I closed his book and returned it to him.

"Did you just read every page?" he asked.

"Why, yes," I said.

"How did you do that? And did you understand any of what was written?"

"I did," I said.

"Everyone, please open your book to chapter twelve." I recited word for word just like it was written on the page. I even had them go to a different page and a different paragraph. I

26

quoted the page just like it was written.

The group sat in awe as I wrote down a problem on the board. At first, they didn't connect to what I was saying until I broke it down. Then a girl who sat in front walked up to the board, wrote her answer to the problem, and sat back down.

"Is she correct?" I asked.

They all agreed that her answer was correct.

I looked at her response. "You are correct."

I did another problem and another. I put up at least ten different problems and asked each student to put their answer on the board.

The class was catching on. Within the next two hours, we worked together to grasp the information presented in the chapter. They all agreed that they had a better knowledge of what chapter twelve was about.

"Let me know after you take your exam what you guys think of my teaching methods."

*****

On our way home, Neala turned her car radio onto a news station. We waited for almost ten minutes before a news story began to broadcast about Cyclone Andrea. It was off the coast of the Island of Catanduanes. "That's not too far from us. Let's go in and get some coffee. We can catch up on what this storm is going to do." After making a pot of coffee, I pulled out food from the freezer. I was hungry for some good ole Sinigang soup. Putting the soup into a large pot, I set it on the stove to heat it up. I heard the front door open. Maria ran towards me, giving me a big hug. I asked, "How was your day?"

"It was good. I read a complete chapter in our reading book and I didn't say any wrong words."

"Thatis fantastic," I said.

My mother and Minda walked in behind her.

Minda put her things down. "Show Ali what your teacher gave you today." Maria removed from her backpack a letter from her teacher.

*"To the parents of Maria Cruz. Miss Maria Cruz has shown extraordinary skills in all of her subjects. She is excelling at a very astonishing rate. We would like to test her to see if she could move up a grade level. We need to get your permission to start assessing her abilities."*

My father walked into the room just as I finished reading the letter. Both of our parent's smiles were as large as they could be. They knew that Minda and I had a helping hand in Maria's school grades.

Minda started setting the dining room table so that we could all eat. I told my parents that Neala would be eating with us every night from now on. They looked up at both of us with a startled expression.

"Are we missing something?" my father asked.

I told them about the situation with the police today, and the news that Neala told me about a drug lord working in the area. My mother was about to take a sip of her soup when she dropped her spoon. Grabbing her napkin, she covered her mouth and cried out, "Not again! Not again!"

Neala spoke up. "Please keep Minda and Maria inside at all times. We don't know what these people are capable of, and I don't want them to harm any of you." My mother got up from the table. We could hear her crying as she ran to her bedroom. My father ran his hands through his hair.

"What are the police doing to catch these people?"

I could tell that Neala was worried. "Everything possible right now. But we don't know when or where they may hit us or someone else. I just got word of this, this morning."

My father locked eyes with Neala. "I know that you'll

protect Ali, and I'll keep an eye on Minda. Christina can watch Maria."

I turned on the television. I wanted to hear about the cyclone off of our coast.

The newscaster started his broadcast. *"Cyclone Andrea has been sitting off the coast of Catanduanes for most of the day. With winds picking up, we may see it turn into a typhoon by early tomorrow morning. Please stay alert in your area. We will update you as soon as we hear from the Emergency Management Dept."*

My father turned to face Neala. "You are welcome to stay here if you would like. The only sleeping arrangements would be the sofa."

"I'm good. I'll stop by early in the morning to check up on Ali."

After Neala had left, I worked with Maria on her homework. My mother appeared from her room several hours later. "Get Maria ready for her bath." Turning, she returned to her room, shutting the door. For the first time that I could ever remember, our house was quiet for the whole night. I didn't say a word to anyone. Minda turned off her night light.

MICHAEL J. ALSUP

# ~Chapter Three~

With no windows in my little schoolroom, I couldn't tell what the weather was up to. I heard the rustling of the tree limbs hitting the school building. This reminded me of the classrooms at the castle. No windows, so there would be no distractions from their studies. The students were going over the assignment on the next chapter in their science class when Neala got up from her chair.

She whispered, "Ladies Room."

"While you are out, can you check on the weather? I think the winds from Typhoon Andrea are beginning to pick up in velocity. We may need to end class early."

Fifteen minutes later, Neala had not returned from the restroom. She always tells me if she's going to be late. I started to worry. I know she can take care of herself, but that doesn't stop the eerie gut feeling that something might be wrong.

"Class, I'm going to use the restroom. Please continue working on the problem I put on the board. I'll be back in a few minutes."

When I opened the ladies room door, I noticed the lights were out. Flipping on the light switch, I saw Neala lying face down on the floor. The only sound I heard was a strong crackling noise, and then my eyes rolled up.

\*\*\*\*\*

I woke up in a small room with several men with guns hanging from their bodies. I tried to sit up, but my head was spinning like a coin flicked with your finger on a table. A large, bearded man in a fancy suit came over to where I was lying. "Good to see you're awake."

"Where am I, and who are you?"

"Names are not important right now. What's important is this, I'm giving you twenty-four hours to produce a better product for me. What I've got isn't working."

Putting my hand against my forehead. "What are you talking about?"

He yanked me off the table I was sitting on. With little effort, he dragged me towards an old, rusty door. As soon as he opened the door, I saw a single light bulb hanging in the middle of the room, casting a low output of light. In the middle of the room, was my sister, Maria, lying on a bed. I screamed at the sight of seeing my little sister, who is now in the hands of the devil. Tears formed in my eyes.

"Why did you take my sister?"

"She's my insurance."

"You will make me my drug, or I'll have her killed in front of you. Do you understand?" This evil man yanked on my arm so hard that I let out a scream. "You're hurting me."

He released my arm only to push me toward another door inside a small damp room. There was a small lab setup where several people with masks covering their faces, were working on some kind of mixture. Donning a lab coat and mask, I stood next to a young woman mixing some kind of chemicals. After talking to her, I found out that this is the stuff that is killing most of the people who have tried it.

These so-called lab technicians dont't have a clue about the human body and what certain chemicals would do when mixed with other chemicals and injected.

"Where are your notes?" I asked.

"What notes?" this dingy woman said.

"How are you mixing this chemical with another chemical, not knowing what it does or if you are using the wrong amount?"

"We were told to mix these two together. Nothing more."

"Oh, great. No wonder you're killing people."

While I watched her mix one powder with another, a tall, slender man with a two-day-old beard walked into the room where we were standing.

"Well, Miss Ali. I see that you're getting the picture of what we're doing."

Turning to face him, "I see that you don't have a clue. This woman doesn't even know what day it is."

"Stop with the insults. You'll hurt her feelings."

"Now, I want you to develop for me a new drug that we can make cheaply. We have a large market of clients waiting for you to produce this for us. I want it in powder form so we can distribute it without it being noticed. You have twenty-four hours, or I will inject your sister with my old drug. Do you understand?"

"Yes," I said.

This man ordered a woman, with a large scar across her face, to stand guard. "If she tries to leave, shoot her and her sister."

I looked around, and everything they had on hand was chemicals, liquids and containers. I worked all day and through the night trying to make an evil product for not one, but two evil human beings. Life means nothing to them. All they care about is money and power over others.

The next morning, both of these men walked into the lab.

"Well, what do you have for us?"

I showed them a white powdery substance.

The fancy-suited man picked up a small sample. "What's it

called?"

"I don't have a clue to what you're going to call it."

"How do you use it?" He asked.

"I guess you can sniff it or heat it into a liquid to make an injection."

"Let's try it," he said.

Taking a small amount, he heated it in a spoon over a Bunsen burner, and then he drew it up into a syringe.

He told the two cops that had stopped Neala and me a couple of days ago to bring Maria in here.

I screamed. "Don't do this to her. She's my sister." He back-handed me across the face knocking me to the floor.

The two men holding Maria, who was already drugged, were being held while this horrible man took his syringe and injected her, then he tossed her onto a nearby cot like she was just trash. Everyone watched her for several minutes. She awoke for just a moment, and then she looked at me for just a second, and that was the last breath she would ever take. A skinny man checked her heartbeat. Looking up at the fancy-dressed man, he stated, "She's dead."

"Find someone else that we can try this stuff on. She was still high on the drugs you gave her last night."

I broke down and cried next to Maria. "What have I done?" I started screaming as loud as I could. "You made me kill her! You made me kill her!" The woman with the scarred face stepped next to me. She stuck a stun gun into my neck.

I was taken to the room that Maria was held in when I saw her for the first time. As I lay there, I could hear noises coming from the other room. I heard the big man tell his men. "Take care of it." Through the walls, I could hear gunfire. My mind was spinning. *'What's going on?'* was all I could think of. I heard several loud shots just outside my door when it was suddenly pushed open with a swift kick.

Standing in the shadow from the light bulb, I knew that it was Neala.

"Ali, are you okay?"

"I am," with a sobbing voice. "They made me kill Maria."

Neala said with a stern voice. "Stay here and do not come out."

I laid there crying and nodded to Neala's command.

Lifting my face upward, I looked around the room. I got to my feet and stumbled towards the darkest corner of the room. I wanted to hide. Suddenly, the door opened with a creaking sound, and standing in the opening, I saw the tall skinny man.

"Come here, Ali, I have something for you." He held a syringe in his hand and let some of the liquid leak out.

He took one more step toward me when Neala came up behind him, snatching the syringe out of his hand and stuck it into his neck, pushing the plunger all the way.

"Enjoy it yourself," she said, giving him a hard kick that sent him flying into the opposite wall. Turning, he stared at Neala. He couldn't believe what had just happened to him. With his eyes opened wide, he slid down the wall with the syringe sticking in his neck.

I hollered at Neala. "Find the man in the fancy suit. He's the drug lord."

"Stay here. Don't say a word to anyone."

Neala left to gather up several agents. "Find the man in a fancy suit. He's the drug lord that started all of this." Everybody began to spread out.

Neala saw a flash through the jungle of a fancy object moving. Running in a different direction, she wanted to head him off. Waiting behind a large tree, she surprised this low life of a human being. Stepping from behind her hiding place, she ordered him with a strong voice. "Drop your weapon!" He put on a calm face and did a foot shuffle. Neala called him again.

"There won't be a next time." He tossed his weapon onto the ground.

Waiting for the other agents to catch up with her, there was a loud noise from a gunshot. Neala felt a painful burning sensation in her right side, that told her she was just hit. Touching her side, she saw blood on her hand. Moving with her cat-like reflexes, she returned fire. Taking out one of the cops that had stopped her days earlier, she knew the other one had to be nearby. Waiting for some kind of sign to the whereabouts of this other man, another shot rang out. That bullet hit a tree limb just above her head. She took off to find a better position, and saw the fancy-suited man picking up his weapon. Neala yelled at him to drop his weapon again. This time he aimed at her. She yelled. "This is for Ali." Neala shot him three times. She then returned fire at the last man.

When he gave up his hiding place, he was surrounded by federal agents. Taken into custody, this so-called two-bit thug-of-a-cop would never be a free man again.

Neala took off her shirt and held it against her wound.

As I'm sitting in the darkest part of the room, tears were flooding my vision. A light came from the door opening for the third time. Neala walked in.

"Ali, are you in here?" Standing up, I ran to her. I made sobering noises. I tried to hug Neala, but she stopped me. Looking at her, she didn't have a shirt on. Then I noticed the blood-stained fabric she was pressing against her side.

Neala was hurt.

"Are you okay?" I asked.

"Never better."

Walking out the main door, several agents tooked Neala's arms and sat her down. One agent made a call to get a helicopter in. "Agent down! Agent down!"

With Neala, Maria's body, and myself, we were loaded onto a helicopter, and the onboard paramedic started to take Neala's vital signs. I locked my eyes on her shirt, it was covered in blood. Watching her face, I saw her eyes rolled upwards. She was unconscious. Looking out the window, there was nothing but jungle and the Mayon volcano in the horizon.

I bowed my head, "Lord, please save my friend. I have already lost so much. I don't know if I can continue on." My spirit has been broken from the loss of life that was so dear and precious to me. The paramedic listened to my voice asking our Lord for help. She didn't say a word. She knew what it was like to lose someone so close to you.

# ~ Chapter Four ~

Watching out the side window of the helicopter, a sign on the building appeared. AGO General Hospital was coming into view. The landing skids had just touched the earth when a crew of nurses and doctors rushed towards the helicopter. Neala was removed and rushed into surgery. Since I didn't have any life-threating injuries, two nurses put me in a wheelchair to be checked out by an emergency room doctor, and Maria's body was taken down to the morgue. I was a total wreak and in shock. I needed to make a phone call to my parents. Checking my pockets, I remembered my phone was taken when I was kidnapped. I asked several people sitting in the waiting room if I could borrow their phone, but most of them didn't have one. A young girl about my age saw me with my reddened eyes, messed up hair, and bloody clothes. She knew that my life had been turned upside down.

With her phone in her hand, she pushed it towards me. "Here, you can use mine," she said.

"Thanks." Sitting down in a waiting room chair, I dialed my father's phone. As soon as I heard his voice, I broke down and cried. My hands were shaking like I had Parkinson's disease. Putting a soaked tissue to my eyes, I couldn't stop the tears from running down my face. After telling him that I was okay, I became hesitant. My sobs became loud. I tried to tell him about Maria, but my throat tightened. After several attempts to give him the information, I could only speak with a soft and fragile voice. That was the hardest thing that I've ever done in my life.

I then told him about Neala being hurt, and she was in surgery. Listening to the noise in the background, my father told my mother about everything that had happened. I gave him my location and asked if he would call Father Bayon. Hanging up the phone, I returned it to the girl standing next to me. I saw that she too had tears in her eyes. While I was using her phone, her family had gotten word from the doctor that her father didn't make it. I wanted to say to them, *"I'm so sorry for your loss."* We looked at each other, but no words were spoken. We both knew the emotional feeling of losing a loved one.

Waiting for my parents to arrive, I returned to a seat next to a wall. Watching a little boy play with his toy, I focused on him and not my problems. He saw my flushed face and tears that kept flowing.

With his small child's voice, he asked, "Are you okay?"

I hesitated in answering him.

Wiping my eyes with my shirt. "Yeah, I'm okay."

With a smile on his face, he brought joy to life instead of the evil I had experienced. "My mommy is hurt. They took her in there." He pointed his little finger at the emergency entrance.

"I hope your mommy is okay."

He turned to walk to the man sitting on the other side of his chair.

My mind went back to my world. There is so much hate and death. I started crying again.

Pulling my feet up against my chest, I wanted to be somewhere else. I shut my eyes to the world around me.

There was a tap on my arm. Waking, I saw my mother's eyes that were red from crying. "Momma," I said, hugging her tightly. She burst into tears seeing that I was still alive. My father and Minda gathered around me.

My father's face was a mess from crying as well. "We were

so scared that we lost you. When I heard your voice, I yelled to your mother you were still alive. We rushed here just as fast as we could. I even got pulled over for speeding. After I told the police officer what the emergency was, he escorted us here."

My mother looked at me from head to toe. "Are you okay? Did they hurt you?"

"I'm okay. They killed Maria in front of me. They wanted a new drug to sell. They forced me at gunpoint to make it for them. Then they injected it into Maria. She was already drugged when they did this to her. She opened her eyes just for a moment. She saw me next to her. She smiled at me, and then she collapsed. She just stopped breathing."

My father was angry now. He raised his voice. I saw the veins on his temples sticking out. "What happened to these monsters?"

"Neala wasn't going to let any of them walk away. She made it her goal to stop this drug lord. She hunted each one and killed them. She was shot trying to take out the last one. Two of them were the police officers that stopped us a few days ago. I think one of them is still alive and in federal custody."

Minda wiped her tears. "I thought we had lost you." I hugged her tight.

"I thought I would never see you again."

My father asked. "Have you heard about Neala?"

"No. I was brought into the emergency room to be checked out. I haven't gone to where Neala was taken."

"Can we go and find her?" I asked.

My mother tried to wipe her tears. "Do you know where they took Maria?"

"They told me she was taken to the morgue."

My mother wiped her eyes with a tissue. Looking at my father, mother insisted. "Please take me to her."

Minda started asking several people how to get to the

morgue. As soon as she was given the directions, we headed there at a fast pace.

Because of our ages, Minda and I were not allowed to enter the morgue. The both of us sat on the floor just outside of the main doors while our parents were taken to where Maria's body was resting. After signing some papers, they saw Maria for the last time.

My mother broke down, crying her heart out again at seeing Maria's lifeless body. My father locked his eyes onto her. He tried to hold it together, to be a strong man, but the death of a loved one will rip your heart out no matter who you are.

I was in no better shape. My mind was a total disaster. I tried to cry some more but I couldn't. I was hurt, angry and mad at what had happened to my family. The trauma that I went through in the last forty-eight hours was the worst thing that ever happened to me. Then I thought about our parents. I didn't want to be in their shoes right now. Losing another daughter would have a major effect on both of them for the rest of their lives.

Minda and I sat there for almost an hour before my parents walked out. I saw my father with his arms around my mother's shoulders. She was traumatized by all the events that has happened.

"Daddy, may I borrow your phone? They took mine and I need to make some calls." He handed me his phone as they walked past us.

"Thanks," I said, wiping away another tear.

He didn't say a word. They just kept walking to the elevators. Minda and I got up and followed behind them.

Riding up to the main floor of the hospital, he walked her to the waiting room. I wiped away what tears I had left and called the president. After dialing, I waited for him to pick up. Then I remembered what he had told me. He would never answer his phone if he hadn't already installed the number. Closing my eyes, I needed to think about what to do in case of an emergency, and I didn't have my secure phone. I sat down and leaned against a wall. I had to keep telling myself to think, think, think. Closing my eyes, I concentrated on the procedure that I needed to remember. Type a message with a code and the word 'Legaspi'. The president's security will decode the message and he will call me back. After entering the information, I hung up. Sitting there feeling so helpless, I closed my eyes.

At first, I didn't recognize the sound of the phone ringing. Then I remembered it was my father's phone. Looking at the display, I answered the incoming call.

Speaking in a choked-up voice. "Mr. President, this is Ali. I'm having to use my father's phone since mine was taken by the drug lord."

"Are you okay, Ali?" he asked. "How's Neala?"

"She's in surgery as we speak. She was shot trying to protect me. She and a group of agents raided the drug lords hideout where my younger sister Maria, and I were kidnapped. Before Neala and the agents were able to take down these bad people, they killed my little sister."

"Oh my," the president said. "Where are you now?"

"We were flown to AGO General Hospital. We're still here. I guess we've been here for several hours already. Not sure about Neala's condition. My parents are here, but they are in bad shape."

"Ali, how are you holding up?"

"I'm doing okay, I guess. Considering what has happened in the last forty-eight hours."

"Stay there, and I will have someone come to be with you until Neala is better. They should be there in the next three to four hours. Be sure to ask them this question about Leyte Gulf. I don't want another disaster to happen." After he hung up, I called Father Bayon.

"Hello, Father."

"Hello, Ali. How are you today?"

"Father, did my daddy contact you for me."

"No, I haven't heard from anyone. What's going on?"

"I need you more than anything in this world right now. Can you come to the hospital?"

"What's happened?" he asked.

I told him about me, Maria, and Neala.

"Why yes, my child. I will be there as soon as I can."

"Thank you, Father." And I started crying again. "I need the Lord's wisdom more than anything right now."

It took less than an hour before Father Bayon walked into the waiting room. Minda and I were sitting holding hands when he approached us. My parents looked at each other, then at us. They got up from their seats and walked to where we were standing. Putting their arms around him, I could hear the sobs from parents whose lives were just ripped apart. Minda and I waited to do the same.

"Hello, Father," I said. Looking up at his face, I saw tears in his eyes. I know he's a priest, but he is still a human being just like the rest of us. He feels the same hurt and pain that we feel.

"Hello, Ali." His voice was not so prominent. "How are you holding up?"

"Okay, I guess, considering everything." He tried to conjure up a smile, but somehow, it didn't show.

The Father rested a hand on my shoulder. "Have you heard anything about Neala?"

"No, not yet. Can you ask someone if there is any news?"

"I'll try," he said.

The Father left to check on Neala's condition.

Minda and I returned to the chairs next to our parents. Unaware, Father Bayon returned. I didn't even feel his touch on my shoulder.

"Ali, I just left Neala. She's in the ICU. The doctor told me that she had lost a lot of blood. Her wound didn't hit any vital organs, which is good news. She's still sedated from surgery. As soon as she wakes up, I'll take you to see her."

"Thank you, Father."

"You're welcome," he replied.

Returning to my chair, I must have fallen asleep on Minda's shoulder. I awoke with a tap on my arm.

"Ms. Cruz. Ms. Cruz." A man in a suit stood in front of me.

"Yes? Who are you?"

"I'm Agent Daniel Tomas. I've been assigned to you."

I thought about what the president told me to ask. "What were the directions to find Legaspi's treasure?" He told me the exact detail that I was looking for."

"What's the status of Neala's condition?"

"She's in the ICU. She's still sedated, but we were told that she should be okay."

The agent sat down next to me.

"I have been going over your case. I'm astonished at what you've accomplished at such a young age." He began speaking to me in Russian. I studied his face while I answered his question. I then changed languages to Japanese. He answered my question. His facial expressions seemed to show that he was impressed with me. I then asked him in Cantonese about the weather. He didn't answer.

"Sorry," he said. "I only know four languages."

I smiled. "I know twelve."

Minda was getting a kick out of me. She asked him in Japanese if he had any orange juice to drink.

He smiled at her. After answering her question in Japanese, she pointed at me and told him that I was the person who gave her the inspiration to study another language. Agent Tomas left me where I was sitting, though he didn't go far. I could see him through the waiting room's window.

I sat there staring at the floor. My mind didn't even think about the class that I had left behind. They must have thought that I just left them without saying a word. I called Mrs. Bautista.

She was a little apprehensive when she heard my voice.

"How are you, Ali?" she asked.

"I'm okay, for now," I said. I then explained what had happened. The line was quiet.

"You know that there is only two weeks left in the school year. When you are ready, come and talk to me. Maybe we can work something out."

"I would like that. I feel like I let the students down who trusted me."

Mrs. Bautista was silent for a second. I'll tell them know what happened.

"Thanks," I said, hanging up the phone, I handed it back to my father. He put it back in his pocket without saying a word. I didn't need to be told what he was thinking. His actions said it all. I left to sit on a park bench outside the emergency room door. The new agent leaned against a wall watching me through the glass panel. I must have sat there for more than an hour.

Father Bayon asked my parents where I went. They didn't have a clue. The new agent who was just inside the entrance door pointed his finger where I was sitting, and Father Bayon walked up to me. "Hey," he said in a soft voice. "May I sit down with you?"

I looked at his face.

"Oh please, Father."

We sat there quiet for several minutes. The Father bowed his head as he put his palms together. "Our Lord knows what you are going through. Please, do not give up. You have suffered a tremendous setback in life. Worse than before."

I looked into the Father's eyes.

"Yes, my child. I know that our Lord heard your prayers."

"Father, my parents are upset with me. My own father won't even speak to me. I feel like I'm the cause of all of this evil and death."

"No, my child. You are not the cause. Evil exists in our world, and it has a way of tearing us apart. There can never be all good or all bad. As human beings, we must deal with it as best as we can. Your father does not hate you. He and your mother's world has been torn apart with the death of Maria. In time, they will come to accept what has happened just as you will. I hope you continue with your teaching."

The Father opened his arms. "There are lots of people who are waiting for your guidance. The world is waiting, for you."

"Thank you, Father, for listening to me."

"You're welcome, Ali. Anytime you need someone to talk to, give me a shout. I'm here for you."

"Thanks again, Father."

I got up from my seat so I could be with my parents. I could hear Minda on her phone talking business with a client.

"Mom, dad, can I talk to you?"

They looked up at me. At first, I thought they were going to send me away. My mother asked me to come closer.

Standing next to her, she hugged me and kissed the top of my head. My father seemed hesitant at first, but he too wrapped his arms around me.

My parents looked at each other, then at me. My father spoke with a soft voice, "Ali, you're still our daughter. We are behind you and Minda one-hundred percent. We know that you did not hurt Maria, but the evil in our world did. We know in our hearts that you are trying to make a better place for all of us. And there are some people who will stop at nothing to get what they want. No matter who gets hurt in the process."

"I just talked to Father Bayon. He says Neala is in the ICU

and is going to make a full recovery."

Minda came up next to me, and I told her about Neala. "That's wonderful news," she said.

Agent Tomas returned to the waiting room. "Daddy, this is Agent Tomas. President Datu sent him to be with me until Neala is better." The two men shook hands.

"Ali, now that I know that you are in good hands, I will take your mother home."

"That's fine, daddy."

"Minda, do you want to stay with me or go home with our parents."

She thought for a second. "I really need to go home. I have a meeting tomorrow with a new client that could mean millions for the company."

"I understand," I said.

Father Bayon, Agent Tomas, and I headed towards the ICU. It was just like before. I was not old enough to go into the room. After showing his badge to the security guard and explaining who was in the ICU room, I was given a pass.

Standing next to Neala's bed, I picked up her hand and held it. Father Bayon walked around to the other side and did the same. We bowed our heads. The Father began a prayer for our dear friend. Grabbing a tissue from the box next to her bed, I cried again. "Sorry, Father. I couldn't hold my tears back any longer."

"No need to apologize," he said, wiping his eyes as well. "Agent Tomas didn't show any emotion towards Neala. He doesn't know her like we do. She's just another agent, nothing more. He will never know how she has become a part of my life, a stepmother, and a big sister."

Father Bayon stayed with us for several more hours, but he too had to leave as well. A nurse brought two chairs for us to sit in. I thanked her for being so kind. She smiled. "If you need anything, just shout. I'm just across the room."

"I will," I said.

# ~Chapter Five~

Neala woke up to see me next to her bed. She smiled, knowing that I was there for her. Tapping my arm, I opened my eyes to see her face. "Hey," I said in a soft voice.

"Hey, yourself." She then saw a man standing on the other side of her bed.

"Who are you?"

"I'm Agent Frank Tomas. I have been assigned to watch Ali since you are hurt."

"I see," Neala responded. "How long have I been here?"

"They brought you in yesterday. I called the president and told him. He had an agent assigned until you're back on your feet. Father Bayon stayed with us for several hours, but he had to leave last night."

Neala studied me. "Ali, how are you doing? Are you holding up to everything that has happened?"

"I guess so. I'm dealing with the loss of Maria the only way I know how. One minute at a time. My parents were here at the hospital for most of the day yesterday. I called the school to let them know what happened to you and me. I will contact the dean again when we are in better condition."

Neala coughed. I watched her hold her side as she gritted her teeth. She pushed the call button on her bedrail.

A nurse walked into the room.

"Can I get some water to drink?"

As soon as the nurse left, I took Neala's hand. "I'm going to go home so I can change clothes and clean up. I'll be back in a few hours. I don't have a cell phone right now. If you need me, you can call my father's phone until I can get a new one."

I didn't want to leave Neala right now, but knowing her, she will be giving the nurses a run to get everything she needed.

*****

When we arrived at our home, I heard my father talking to someone about the funeral arrangements. Seeing my mother preparing lunch, I made sure that she saw Agent Tomas and me. She gave me a slight smile while she cut up the vegetables.

Standing in the kitchen leaning against a door frame, I watched her prepare a meal. "Neala is awake. I came home to take a bath and change clothes."

My mother was glad to see me home again. "I should have lunch ready when you are finished."

The four of us sat in silence while we ate our lunch. I didn't know how hungry I was until I sat down to this wonderful meal.

"Minda is at the office," my father said as he got up to put his dishes into the sink.

"I'm glad that she has taken the job. She will do well into the future." After eating, I cleaned up the table and did the dishes.

"I'm going back to the hospital to check on Neala. I'm not sure when I'll be back."

My mother just waved her hand as we walked out of the door.

*****

The ICU nurses taking care of Neala, had just left her bedside when Tomas and I opened her curtain. In a sarcastic voice, "They are moving me to a private room."

"That's good news," I said.

Agent Tomas and I hung around with Neala in the ICU, waiting for the nurses to show up. I heard some commotion just outside her room. Three nurses threw open the curtain that surrounded Neala's bed and began to gather up Neala's belongings. The bed was unplugged, and the wheels were unlocked. Siderails were pulled up on each side of Neala. Moving out of the way, Neala's bed was rolled out of the ICU.

Following her, we stayed back away from her bed as she was wheeled to a stepdown unit and into another room. As soon as the nurses had everything set up, we walked in. Handing her a soda from a vending machine, Neala smiled.

Taking a sip, "Oh man," she said. "That's wonderful. I've only had water to drink."

I updated Neala on everything that had happened to this point.

"As soon as you are ready to take on the world again, I want to go back to the school to check in on the class."

Neala smiled. I think she liked the idea that she would still be my bodyguard.

Neala was laid up in her hospital bed for almost a week. Arriving on a Saturday morning, Agent Tomas and I found Neala putting the finishing touches on her wardrobe.

"Where to?" I asked.

"I need to see if my car is still at the school," she said.

Agent Tomas pulled his car up to the front of the hospital. With gritted teeth, Neala climbed into the front passenger side of his car. The three of us took off, hoping that we would never have to stay here ever again. Not that it's a bad place to be. It's just a hospital.

\*\*\*\*\*

We found Neala's car just where she had left it. The only thing she was missing was her sidearm, cellphone, and badge.

Agent Tomas made a call. After talking to his supervisor, he hung up. "Neala, you're going to have to go to the office in Manila to retrieve your things."

Neala stared out the side window as we headed away from the hospital.

"Ali, I have something very important to do. May we go to your home?"

"Oh, sure," I said.

Neala followed Agent Tomas and me home. I kept quiet with my thoughts. '*Why does Neala want to go to my house?*'

When I opened our door, Neala asked. "Ali, can you go get your parents?" I found my mother in the kitchen, and my father was in the backyard repairing something.

They both appeared in front of Neala and me.

"What's up?" my father asked.

Neala put her hands together. "I wanted to say that I am sorry about the way things happened to your family. I let my guard down, and it cost a precious little girl her life. I was so excited to see Ali teaching college students that I let someone attack her while she was at school. This would have never happened if I had been vigilant with my job of protecting her. I have to return to Manila. I'm not sure if I will still have a job when I get there. Agent Tomas will be watching Ali."

My father listened to Neala, but in his mind, she would be the one who would be watching over me. "Neala, if you are relieved from your duties working for the government, you can start your own private security company here. Watching over Ali will be your assignment, and I will pay your salary."

"Thank you, Mr. Cruz, for your confidence in me. It's been

bothering me ever since I awoke from surgery. When is Maria's funeral?"

"It's tomorrow at the St. Rose of Lima Parish Church. Father Bayon will be handling the service."

"My orders are to return to Manila tonight. Ali, have you bought a new cell phone?"

"No, not yet," I said.

"Okay, get one as soon as you can. Your father has my number. He can call me before I lose my job, and this cell phone. I will purchase another one in Manila, if need be. I want to know where you are at all times."

"Okay," I said with a smile. I didn't want to lose Neala because of some evil person wanting to harm me. She was attacked from the back, just like me.

*****

Maria's funeral was beautiful. Father Bayon came over to where my family was gathered, putting his arms around us and asked us to pray with him.

I don't think that there was a dry eye in the church. My family saw Maria's beautiful face for the last time. I stood next to her when Father Bayon said one last prayer over her. The casket's lid was closed. We thanked everyone for attending Maria's funeral and said goodbye as they began to leave. With everything that has happened, I didn't see Dr. Montoya at the service. He walked over and stood next to me.

"Ali, are you still the CEO of your company or have you started teaching somewhere?"

"I gave up my position, and now, Minda is CEO."

The doctor smiled, "I thought that may happen if you ever decided to leave."

"How old is Minda now?"

"She's eleven. She received her bachelor's degree at the age of nine."

"My, my. That's impressive," he said.

"What are your plans now?"

"I may still have a position at Zamora College, but it's not permanent."

"Ali, you have my number. Call me."

"I'm afraid I don't have a cell phone as of right now. It was taken from me when I was kidnapped."

Dr. Montoya gave me his business card. "When you get another one, call me so we can discuss about you teaching. I am convinced that you could teach any student and take them to the highest level of achievement."

# ~Chapter Six~

First thing on my to do list was to purchase a new cell phone. Plugging it into Agent Tomas' car charging port, I sat watching the battery meter move at a snail's pace. It took a long agonizing fifteen minutes to even begin to show a small charge. I called Neala's number. I hoped she would answer my call, but she never did. Thinking aloud. *"They must have taken her phone from her by now."*

I looked at Agent Tomas. "Neala is not answering her phone."

He made a call to his supervisor asking about Neala. After several minutes, I watched him as he hung up.

"Neala has been relieved of her duties as an agent with the government. They have put me in charge of watching over you."

"Nothing personal, but I'm not so sure that this is going to work out."

I dialed the president's personal cell phone. I knew his phone is set up to not answer unkown phone numbers, so I went through the same steps as before.

After my number was run through a security system to make sure that I was legit, he returned my call.

"Ali, it's good to hear from you."

"Mr. President, Neala has been terminated from her job. I've been assigned another agent, but I'm not too sure if it's going to work out. My father has asked Neala to be my personal bodyguard. If she accepts, then I won't need a government agent to watch over me."

"I see. I'll look into this matter. But there's not much I can do about the decision that's been made."

"I understand. I'll make my own decision as to the agent's future with me. Can you make sure that Neala can carry a weapon anywhere in the country, if she starts her own personal security company?"

"I'll see what I can do."

"Thanks, Mr. President. That would be helpful."

I kept my call short and to the point. Trying to get in touch with Neala right now would be useless. I'll just have to wait and see if she shows up at my door.

*****

The following morning, Agent Tomas was sitting outside my house in his car when my parents, and Minda left to go to the office, I waved at him.

"You can come in and have some coffee, if you would like."

"That would be great."

As we sat there making small talk, I heard a knock on my door. I watched Agent Tomas put his hand on his pistol. He got up from his chair putting his back on the open side of the door frame.

Standing to the other side of the door, I yelled. "Who is it?"

"It's Neala."

I recognized her voice. I couldn't open the door fast enough. She stood there with an empty coffee cup. I wrapped my arms around her and gave her a big hug.

"Got any coffee?"

"I sure do." Taking her cup to wash it out, I then filled it up for her. I was gleaming with joy at seeing her again.

Agent Tomas looked at Neala. "It's good to see you again."

"Thanks. My situation of making it through this ordeal was close."

"Ali, you know that I'm no longer employed with the government."

"Yeah, I know. Agent Tomas checked up on your status. If you would like to work for us, my father has already stated that he would hire you as a full-time security officer. Your pay would be considerably more."

Agent Tomas studied Neala's face. "That sounds like a good deal. One that would be very hard to pass up."

"It does at that." She thought for a moment. "I'll have to get a security clearance to carry a weapon."

"Did you buy another phone?" I asked.

"I did. Here's my new number." Putting it into my phone, I called hers. Now, she has mine. I also put Agent Toma's number in mine as well. "You never know who you may need to call." Neala did the same.

"Oh, I also called President Datu. I told him your situation and asked if he could check into getting you a clearance to carry a weapon throughout the country."

"Thanks, Ali. Any help is always a good thing."

Neala borrowed my laptop to check on acquiring a security license. While she scanned a bunch of websites, my phone rang.

It was President Datu.

"Ali, have you heard from Neala?"

"I have, sir. She is sitting next to me."

"May I speak with her?"

I handed my phone to Neala.

"Neala, I need your new phone number. And I'm texting you a small document that you will need to carry with you. It will get you around all the red tape of getting a security license. You will be able to carry and protect Ali. I would still go and get a security license so there won't be any problems later."

'I will, sir, and thanks for believing in me."

"You're welcome, Neala."

After hanging up, Neala turned towards me. "Do you have a Bluetooth printer?"

"I do," getting up to turn it on.

Neala made the connection and printed out her new document.

"This solves one of your problems. It's the start of your new career."

"It is at that," she said.

With the help from Agent Tomas, Neala didn't have to go through all of the red tape that a person would have to go through to get a security badge, and be able to carry a weapon. She was issued a license.

*****

I had supper ready when my parents and Minda wandered in. With our table set for two extra people, though our home was small, it still serves us well.

My parents could buy a larger house, but we have made a lot of memories here. One day, Minda and I will grow up and someday move on to make our own life.

After eating, my father needed some answers from Neala.

"Neala, what are your plans for today and the future?"

She hesitated for a second. "I just received my security license, and I received a special note from President Datu so I can carry it throughout the country."

"That's wonderful news," my father said.

"I need to ask you if you would consider watching over Ali. I think she wants you to be her bodyguard."

Neala already knew my answer.

My father smiled. "You can start your own company just like you did at the plant. I'll get you a company credit card so you can make purchases, if warranted. And, I'll increase your salary from what you were making with the government."

"Since I don't have a job at this moment, I would like to work for you."

"Can you start today, right now?"

"Yes sir. That would be great." My father reached in his pocket and gave her a so-called sign on bonus of many thousands of pesos.

"This will help you obtain anything that you may need."

"Thank you, sir, it will come in handy."

"Now that all the mussy stuff is over, let's do a toast to Neala, for joining our family."

The six of us clanged our glasses together in celebration.

Agent Tomas got up from our table. "I need to take care of some things. Ali, if you ever need anything, you have my number. Don't hesitate to call. I don't live too far from here and I can come to help out or send for help."

Neala couldn't have agreed more. Sometimes it takes extra services to get the job done.

"Thanks," I said and giving him a hug as he opened the front door.

# ~Chapter Seven~

Thinking to myself, I have decided to find and educate people who have exceptional minds that live outside the cities or towns within my province and maybe in my country. My idea is is to teach others among their own villages or communities. This task alone will be monumental to achieve. Traveling around the Albay Province with Neala, we drove to a number of outlying areas. Some areas, we had to park Neala's SUV and walk for several kilometers into the jungle just to get to a village of people. I was in awe to find out how many students don't go to school or there are no schools available for them to attend. In this modern age of space travel, sending humans to the moon, the Philippines still have a primitive education system. To my way of thinking, that's not good enough. Educating the populous is one way we can help to better their lives as we move into the twenty-first century.

After making a survey about my findings of the limited education or lack of, I compiled a list of areas that would need to be first on my list. While looking over the list, my cell phone rang.

It was Dr. Montoya. "Ali, I read your notes that you sent over from your recent trip to the outlying areas of the province. Can you meet me at my office tomorrow, say about two o'clock? I'd like to discuss the prospects of putting teachers throughout the Albay Province."

I liked the idea, but deep down in my heart, I knew that this was going to be a daunting challenge at minimum.

I placed a call to Father Bayon.

"Ali, how are you? I haven't seen you in church lately."

"I know, Father. I've been out of town a lot. The reason I'm calling is Dr. Montoya wants to have a meeting about putting teachers into the outlying areas of our province."

I could hear the Father rustling papers in his hands. "I see. Now, that would be a major challenge for you."

"He wants to meet tomorrow at two p.m. at his office. Can you make this meeting?"

"Give me a moment to check my calendar." I could hear more rustling of papers. "I can be there."

"That's great. See you tomorrow."

*****

Opening the door to Dr. Montoya's office with Neala by my side, his secretary looked up from the papers she had piled up on top of her desk.

"May I help you?"

"We have a meeting with Doctor Montoya," I said.

"And may I ask who's calling?"

"Ali Cruz and Neala."

She picked up her phone. "Sir, a Miss Ali Cruz and Neala is here to see you."

"Send them in."

"You may go in," she said.

"Thank you," I replied.

Entering his office, I saw Father Bayon was already there. Putting his right hand to my forehead. "Good afternoon, Father."

"Ali, so nice to see you again."

Dr. Montoya waved his hand at the other two chairs.

"Please sit down. Okay Ali, tell me what your future plans are."

"Well, I have resigned as CEO of my company and I am going to pursue my dream of teaching."

The doctor studied me with his large eyes. Rubbing his joules with his right hand, he swiveled his chair slightly so he could look away. Pausing for just a moment, he turned to face me. Gazing into my eyes, it seemed as though he could read my mind.

"Okay, I can relate to what you're telling me. I have always wondered when you would decide to follow your heart." Standing up, he walked from behind his desk and stood next to a large window. I can see a classroom full of students with an IQ that Einstein would be jealous of. "So, when are you planning to start your newest project?"

"I had just started teaching a small group of students at Zamora College when my world fell apart. I haven't gone back to check to see if my position there had changed. I think it would be in my best interest to start planning to start my own school. Just like before, I'm going to have to find a building that will house the classroom as well as the students."

"So, where are you wanting to set this up?"

"I would like to set up here in Bacacay. It would bring more jobs to our area. We will need to have personnel to maintain the building and run the kitchen for the students. I will ask President Datu if the government would help in covering the cost of running such a school."

"Don't count on the government to give you a lot of help. The red tape is enormous."

"I know. Just like before. We had to do our own thing to get my business up and running."

"Ali, if you don't mind, can you call me by my name. My name is Med Montoya. My friends call me Med."

"Okay, Med. Do you have any buildings that may work for us?"

"Well, I own several buildings. You are welcome to look at any of them." Opening a desk drawer, he produced a list of buildings.

"Here are all my properties in different cities and towns around the Albay Province. I'll have my secretary make a copy of everything on this list. You can check out any of them and then we will talk again. As we have discussed in the past, I am very keen on teaching the people in our country and provide a form of higher education. I want to see more Filipino doctors, especially neurosurgeons, oncologists, etc, being taught right here. I would love to see the Philippines as one of the most prestigious countries in the world for medicine. I will personally put in two million US dollars to get your project off the ground. And if you like, I have a CPA who can run the financials as well."

I looked at the doctor's face. "That's a really good start. Once I choose a building, I will contact you as before to discuss our future." Neala was silent during this meeting. I saw the look on her face and I knew that she does not like to be left out of anything that I am involved in.

"Neala will head up the security of our school. She has her own security business and is very good at her job." I caught the slight turn up of her lip.

Dr. Montoya's secretary walked into his office handing me the list of buildings for sale.

"Neala and I will check out your properties and get back with you in a few days."

Med smiled at me. "Sounds good."

We got up to leave when Med and Father Bayon got up from their chairs. Father Bayon moved over to where I was standing. "Ali, if you need anything, please let me know. I would like to help you anyway I can."

Neala glanced my way as soon as we got into her SUV.

"What are our plans for today?" she asked.

"Are you up to doing a little looking?" I asked. Pulling out my notebook, I removed the list that we had just received. There are twenty-two properties to look at.

Neala glanced my way.

"Let's take the farthest one out and work our way back to here."

"That sounds like a plan to me," I said.

Our first stop was not too productive. The building though seemed big enough, but it was in terrible shape. The cost alone would be prohibitive.

"I think this one's a bust."

Neala looked my way. "I think you're right. Let's move on."

The next two weren't any better. Sitting in Neala's SUV, she heard my stomach growl.

"Are we getting hungry?" she asked.

Putting on my best smile. "I am."

"How does Angelica's Pizza sound?"

With her Mango shake, she said, "Oh yeah, I'm in." Pulling up to the restaurant, we were greeted with Angie's beautiful smile. After ordering a large pizza and two shakes, we dove into this delicious meal.

Looking at our list, Angie became curious about what we were up to. I explained what my plans were and how Dr. Montoya was helping me with my search for property to buy.

She studied me while we ate our food. Making her way to our table, she smiled. "Let me make a phone call." Several minutes passed before Angie returned to where Neala and I were seated. "I have a cousin that has a hotel that he closed and wants to sell the property." I became excited.

"Where is it located?"

"It's in Legaspi City."

"Do you have an address?"

Neala wrote down the information. After paying our bill, we were both kind of curious about this hotel for sale. I thanked Angie for her help, and we left.

Getting into Neala's SUV, we headed towards Legaspi. Making our way around just about every kind of vehicle or people walking along the road, we finally stopped at the gates of the Seafare Hotel. Peering through the gates ornament, I saw what seemed to be five floors high and guessing twelve bedrooms across each floor.

Neala peered through the gate as well. "This is nice."

"I wander how much they're asking for it." Pulling my cell phone out of my back pocket, I called Med. I explained to him about the hotel and how we found out about it from Angie.

"Let me make some calls."

After a fifteen-minute wait, my phone rang.

"Ali, the owners are asking three-million US dollars for the place."

"I see. It would serve our purpose, but it is way out of our price. Thanks for checking." Neala and I continued looking at the properties on Dr. Montoya's list.

We looked at another dozen buildings, but I was not in favor of any of them. Most of them needed a lot of repairs and renovation. Neala could tell by my facial expression that it was time to call it a day. Pulling up to the front of my house, we sat in her SUV staring out the windshield.

"We can check out what's left on the list tomorrow," she said.

"Sounds like a good plan," I said.

"Pick you up at eight."

Opening the front door, I saw my parents and Minda sitting at the dinner table. I guess I didn't hide my disappointment too well.

My mother gave me her parent look. "Wash up and eat."

Sitting at our table, my mother set a plate of food in front of me.

My father watched me stirring the food on my plate, "Rough day?"

"Yeah, kinda. It started out being promising except one of the properties that Angie told me about in Legaspi was nice, but way out of my league. Dr. Montoya checked into the asking price and the owner wants three-million US dollars for it."

"What is the name of the property?"

"It's called the Seafare Hotel."

My father smiled. "I've stayed there before when I worked at my old job. It's a really charming hotel."

"Neala and I could only see it from the closed gates, but from what I could see, it would serve very well to house students that are expecting to attend my school."

My mother turned to face me from the kitchen sink,

"You have high hopes that you can fill it up with students. That's what dreams are made of, high hopes." She just smiled returning back to doing the dishes.

Minda sat quiet the whole time I had this conversation with my parents.

"Is there anything I can do to help?" she asked.

"Not yet. But if and when I can get this school put together, I can use your great mind to help teach. There should be students from every walk of life and age group. You'll be the inspiration to help them push themselves to the next level of their education. I witnessed this with my very own eyes when you received your B.S. Diploma from the University of the Philippines."

Minda smiled. "This would have never happened without you."

I squeezed her shoulder as I walked by her. I knew that we were bonded as much as two friends could ever be. "I know your time will be limited with your new position at our company."

She looked up at me. "I will do what I can."

"Thanks," I replied.

# ~Chapter Eight~

Scanning our list of buildings, we had seven left to look at. Entering the address of Building Number Sixteen into the GPS, Neala put her SUV into motion. Fifteen minutes later, we sat in front of an old warehouse. Looking at a derelict building, we looked at each other.

"Nah, I don't think so." I had a funny feeling come over me. "It's as old as the castle we stayed in Switzerland." Neala put on a happy face. "Yep. You may try to climb those old stairs, but you may never get down them either."

Smiling at our demeanor, "What's next?"

Buildings thirteen through twenty-one were not usable as a school either. Heading to our last stop, Building Number Twenty-Two, my phone rang. It was Dr. Montoya.

"Ali, how far on the list have you gotten to?"

"We are heading to the last one."

"Forget about it. Meet me at this address…."

Writing down the information, I noticed that it was the Seafare Hotel.

"Okay. What's up?" I asked.

"Just meet me there in thirty-minutes."

Standing next to his vehicle, Med smiled as we pulled up next to his car. Neala turned off her engine as I got out with eagerness to greet him.

Med smiled. "Well, let's talk business. Ali, my good friend,

I just purchased this hotel for our school."

I must have had a dumb look on my face, "Did you say that you just purchased this hotel for our school?"

Med smiled graciously at me. "I did."

My face was so full of joy, my cheeks were burning.

"Ali, do you know the name your school will be called?"

"Not yet. I've been so busy trying to find a new location that I haven't thought about it."

"Well, when you come up with a name, call me so I can draw up the papers with your name and mine, and the schools name. We will get a tax break from the government." I walked over to Dr. Montoya and gave him a hug. He looked down at my face, "Here now, there is no need to cry."

"They're tears of joy," I said between sobs. "I had a dream that someday I'd be able to teach others. You have made my dream come true. Thank you for everything."

"Ali, you are like a daughter to me that I've never had. If I ever have a child, I would want them to have a heart for the human race like you do. This human emotion is very sacred to me."

"May we go and check out the buildings?"

"Oh my, yes. Here are the keys to the front door. I also have other sets to different areas." The three of us walked into the front lobby.

Med pointed at the lights on the wall. "The electricity is not on as of yet, but by the time you return, they will be working. Now, let's see what we can do with this beautiful building." Neala held my hand as we walked together looking at each and every room.

Counting every bedroom, there are sixty rooms for the students. I also noticed that each room still contained all of its furniture. Checking the bathrooms, the only thing missing were towels and toiletries.

Neala smiled. "Very nice. These will do very well for the students." After visiting every room, Dr. Montoya handed me the keys. "Ali, you will need to go to your bank and set up an account under the schools name. Then I will transfer two-million US dollars into the account so you can buy the necessary things to get the school started. Also, contact your lawyer to set up this new business. Let me know when you have your side of the business done. We will also need to set up our school with the Board of Education. They may send a representative here to check you out. So be aware."

"I will. Thanks for everything. I want to tell Father Bayon about our new school."

Med opened the door to his SUV, "I think you're right. Letting the Father know would be a wonderful thing for our future." After Med left, I called my own father to let him know what had just happened. He was in awe that Dr. Montoya was so generous. "If there is anything that you need, just let me know."

"I will daddy. Please tell momma and Minda. Neala and I are still at the hotel building. I think that I am still in a dream and this is just not happening to me."

"No, my dear, you are very much awake, and our Lord is providing you the things that he has plans for."

"I think you are right daddy. I must go and see Father Bayon."

"Ali, I think you should. I will talk to you later."

"Okay," I said as I was hanging up.

*****

Pulling in the parking lot of Saint Rose of Lima Parish Church, I saw Father Bayon doing his daily chores of cleaning the Chapel.

"Hello, Father," I said with a vibrant voice.

"Well, hello Ali. It's good to see you again. So, what brings you here today?"

"May we sit for a moment?"

"Why, of course. I'm sorry Neala. Where are my manners? It's good to see you too."

"I'm fine, Father," Neala said.

"Father, Dr. Montoya has purchased a hotel building just outside Legaspi and has given me the keys. This will be our new school. It has sixty rooms for the students and has several large rooms that can be divided into classrooms. There is also a restaurant where meals will be served."

"My, my. That sounds wonderful. Do you have a name for your new school?"

"No, not yet. My mind is wondering about that very thought. Do you have any ideas?"

"Well, let me think for a second. Hum. How about the School of "Advanced Studies of Higher Education?"

"ASHE," I said.

I thought about the name the Father had just came up with. After several moments, I smiled. "I like it. It does hit the nail on the head, sort of speaking."

Father Bayon looked at my face. "It does do that now, doesn't it?"

"Father, can you come over to our new building and do a blessing over it? It would mean a lot to me, my family, and Dr. Montoya."

"I would love to do a blessing for you. What day and time do you have in mind?"

"Is you schedule open for Thursday morning, say ten o'clock?"

"That would be fine," he said.

"That's wonderful. I will let Dr. Montoya and my family know."

As soon I was buckled in Neala's SUV, I made a call to Med. "I have a name for our school. Father Bayon came up with it. It will be named ASHE. Which stands for Advanced Studies of Higher Education." There was a pause on the phone line.

Med's bold voice came on the line. "I like it. It does have a ring to it, doesn't it?"

"It does at that. Also, Father Bayon will be coming by on Thursday at ten a.m. to do the blessing of our school."

"That's wonderful. I'll see you then."

I placed a call to my father. "Daddy, can you come by to the Seafarer Inn and take a look at it with me?"

"I would love to," he said.

"Also bring Momma and Minda with you, okay?"

"I will see you about five-forty-five."

"Sounds good," I said.

While Neala and I had some time to kill, we went to the courthouse in Legaspi City to get any architectural drawings of the hotel. With this information, I can see if there are any changes to the rooms that I would like to make.

Sitting back in the hotels' front lobby, I saw my father's SUV pull into the driveway. I was watching Minda get out of the backseat, when I saw her look up at the new building with approval. Walking to the lobby, I thought I would put a little tease into the mix. "Good afternoon ladies and gentlemen, I hope your trip to our beautiful hotel was enjoyable."

Minda took the que. "It was just superb," she said. Giggling.

"Please sign in at the front desk and Neala will take your luggage up to your rooms." Everyone laughed at my joke.

"Daddy, Neala and I just came back from City Hall with a copy of the blueprints of the hotel."

"Good thinking. You may need them if you want to make any changes to the rooms or add anything to the property."

"Also, I have Father Bayon coming over Thursday at ten

a.m. to do a blessing of the buildings. Dr. Montoya will be here as well. Can you bring everyone with you to be with us?"

My mother loved hearing what I had planned. "We would love to."

"Thanks daddy. That would mean a lot to me. Everyone, would you like to see the other buildings on the property."

They all said, "Yes."

After we did a walk-through, my father looked at me and inquired, "Have you made any plans for converting this hotel into a school?"

"Not yet. I'm going to notify the Albay School Board and they will probably want to send someone to see the building for themselves. We will have to fill out paperwork to make the school creditable with the Education Dept. If and when we get certified, then I can start making the necessary changes to the buildings as required. We need to add furniture, check the air conditioners in each room and throughout the other buildings, then the fire dept. needs to do an inspection, then afterwards, we will be able to obtain the proper permits to open our school. Of course, I have to advertise throughout the country to see if there are any students who would like to study here. I will personally have to go out into the province and see if there are any students who want to come and learn here. If I only have twenty students to start with, I can teach them as a group, but if there are more students than I can handle, another teacher will need to be hired. I will also be needing a secretary to handle the school's records that must be kept up with to satisfy the school board requirements. We will also have to feed the students, so I will need several cooks and maintenance personnel to take care of any building problems that might spring up."

My father looked down at me. "Ali, you have taken on a project that usually requires a large number of personnel just to get the grassroots started."

"I know daddy, but I'm not afraid of taking on a large challenge."

Neala just smiled. "Amen to that."

\*\*\*\*\*

Thursday morning, Neala and I watched as everyone I invited, arrive at the blessing. Dr. Montoya had just walked into the lobby.

"Good morning, Ali."

"Good morning, Med. I wanted to let you know that I have the Board of Education coming here Monday morning at ten-thirty."

"Dealing with any government bureaucracy can be a pain," he said.

"After I made a call to the education department, they requested a meeting in Manila."

"What time and date?" Med asked.

"Thursday, September the Sixteenth at nine a.m." Neala made a mental note of my plans.

"That gives me about three weeks to get everything I need in place. The name of the school, its location, how many students will be attending, and how many teachers will be working here. Will they be living on campus or off? Is it private or public? And how much are the tuition fees?"

Father Bayon came by our new-to-be-school-building and gave the Lords 'blessing.'

Med and I are grateful for this. We both agreed that it was going to be a great task just to get started. I had everyone gather around Med and myself.

"I would like to thank Father Bayon for giving us the Lord's blessing on taking on this project that had never been done before in the Albay Province."

"Just like before, we took matters in our own hands and believed enough in ourselves to tackle this job that most said could not be done. But we are doing it. This new challenge at hand will test me once again. Can I believe in something so much that I'm willing to bet everything on it?" Med and I took the first step. "We now have a place to have school." There were cheers from everyone.

On our way back home from our meeting with Dr. Montoya, I told Neala about my thoughts and if she had any ideas. Neala glanced over at me. "Let me think about this and I'll get back with you."

Sitting outside of my house in Neala's SUV, she made a call to President Datu. We sat there while Neala was put on hold for several minutes. She put the call on speaker phone, and as soon as he returned, she told him about me being on speaker with her.

"Hello, Ali. It's good to talk to you again."

"Hello, Mr. President. I hope you are doing well."

"Things are good, Ali. What can I help you with?"

"I'm starting up a new school similar to what I attended in Switzerland. I want to start teaching, so I will be looking for students of any age or religious beliefs."

"That is a very tall order," the President said.

"I know. Our students rank incredibly low in the world when compared to other countries. I want to do better than that. I have a meeting with the Board of Education on Tuesday, September the Sixteenth. I need to get the school board's approval before I can proceed."

"I know what this means to you and what you can do for our country. I will make some calls."

"Thank you, Mr. President," hanging up the phone.

\*\*\*\*\*

Standing in front of the receptionist desk at the education department, Neala pointed at a plaque on the wall. It had my picture on it and a short script about me. I smiled as I read it.

*"At the age of four, this remarkable young lady was given the gift of knowledge by our Lord and Savior Jesus Christ."*

A short woman of about forty gave me a quizzical stare. "May I help you?" she said.

"I have an appointment with the Educational Board," I said.

"Your name?"

"Ali Cruz and this is Neala."

The receptionist looked at me. "I don't have her name on my list."

I quickly acknowledged. "She's my bodyguard. She has been assigned to me by the President of the Philippines."

The secretary picked up her phone. After a short conversation, the receptionist looked at me. "Mrs. Vega will be with you shortly. Please have a seat." We had just sat down when a tall slender woman walked up to me.

"You must be Ali. Will you follow me to my office?" As I got up, Mrs. Vega saw Neala getting up with me. "Only Ali needs to be present. You can continue to wait out here."

Neala was not going to have any of this back seat-approach.

"I beg your pardon. Ali does not go anywhere without me." This woman didn't expect Neala to be so protective.

"Well, I never."

"Either I go with Ali or we leave, and you can ask the president why you just lost your job."

The three of us stood at the office door while Mrs. Vega scanned Neala's ID badge. Neala stepped back away from me while I sat in front of Mrs. Vega's desk. After recomposing herself, she sat down.

"I don't think I've ever had a child sitting in my office before. Now what can I help you with?"

"Well for starters, I like the plaque about me that hangs on your wall behind the receptionist desk."

Mrs. Vega had to think about what I just said. "That's you?" she asked.

"It is. I'm starting a school in Legaspi City, in the Albay Province. I will be teaching students from all different academic levels. The knowledge they gain will make the Philippines stand out among all the countries in the world. I would like to see some of the students take their skills to the outlying provinces in our country so they too can teach others who may have some schooling."

"That's quite a tall order," Mrs. Vega said.

"Yes, I know. That was the exact thing President Datu told me. I have a building already. Your department is supposed to come by on Monday and check it out. Before I can start hiring workers, I need to get a certification from the board, then I can proceed on finding students."

"What's your school's name?" she asked.

"It will be called ASHE which stands for Advanced Studies of Higher Education."

"I will go over what you have told me. After we receive the report from the field agent about your building, I will call a board meeting to discuss your plans."

Looking at her with a serious and professional glance, I stated, "You may need to call the president. He will verify everything that I have told you."

# ~Chapter Nine~

Neala and I sat in the main office of our new building waiting for the school board inspector to pay us a visit and give me the great news that I wanted to hear. I was having my doubts about getting the certifications we needed to open our school. In the back of my mind, something just kept nagging me. I feel like I'm missing something but, for the life of me, I couldn't bring it out. With the passing of Maria, my thoughts have not been on my agenda to move this project forward. I hate the wait time when I have to depend on someone else. They may move at their normal pace but when I have to just sit around and not be productive, these things start to get under my skin.

Chatting about our future, Neala asked. "What kind of students are you looking for?"

I thought for a moment. "At first, I was only going to take the upper achievers from our province, but that idea is not sitting too well with me. There are so many students out there that would jump at the chance to have a good education. We have met so many families who would love to have their children grow up and be productive in their lives. But they just don't have the funds to send their kids to school or the means of transporting them to and from school everyday. If I could teach them, then my school will become a success in the community as well as in the country."

Neala took a sip of her coffee.

"I know that I'm going to have to limit the amount of students to work with. I was thinking about taking on just thirty to start."

Taking a sip from my coffee cup, we heard the front door open. Neala stepped out first with her hand resting on her pistol. She went in cautious mode.

She noticed a young gentleman standing at the front desk.

"May I help you?" She asked.

"I'm looking for Ali Cruz. I'm with the Board of Education."

I stepped around the desk. He seemed a little apprehensive to talk to a person of my age.

He stumbled with his speech. "I'm looking for Ali Cruz," he said again.

"I'm Ali Cruz. Are you here to inspect my buildings?"

"I am. I will need to see all of your property. Then I need a list of everything that you will be teaching. How many students, counselors, and teachers will be working here? Also, will the students be staying here or will they live off these premises."

While he was talking, I made notes of everything he asked for. Neala just smiled as we walked to every room.

Standing next to this Board of Education representative, I looked up at his face. "I will also hire caretakers as well, and a full staff of chefs."

His body language told me that I was not ready to open a school.

I looked at him with a professional face. I know my building is ready. I will hire people to fill these positions.

He made some notes. "You hire the staff that it takes to run a school like this, and I'll come back and inspect your buildings again. Here's my card. And here is a copy of my notes. Call me when you have the personnel on your payroll.

I thanked him for coming over.

As the front door shut, it hit me. How could I be so stupid?

I haven't even gone over to the bank to setup the account for my school. I won't be able to hire anyone without a bank account to buy products or services that I may need.

Neala just stood there smiling.

I caught the look on her face. "What are you smiling about?"

"I'm watching one of the most intelligent humans on the planet, just being human. We all make mistakes."

Shutting the office door. "I know that's right." I mumbled.

"Neala can you take me over to the bank? I was wondering how you were going to pay for the things you are going to need."

I began my ranting again. "How stupid of me. I wanted to open this school, like yesterday."

As soon as we entered the bank, the same secretary that sat in the front the last time I wanted to open an account, noticed me.

"Hello Ms. Cruz. How may we help you?"

"I want to open a new account for a school that I'm starting." She gave me some papers to fill out about the new business. After I had completed them, she called the bank manager.

Mr. Reyes walked over to his secretary's desk. "Hello, Ms. Cruz. How are you today?"

"I'm fine. I'm opening a new account for a school that I am starting up. Dr. Montoya will be depositing two million US dollars into it."

"Will he be on the Board of Directors?"

"He will," I said.

Mr. Reyes looked at me. "And will he have access to the funds."

"I would think so," I said.

"Then he'll need to come by and sign some papers."

"That's fine. I'll call him and let him know."

"Also Ms. Cruz, since you are still under the age of eighteen, we will need a signature from your parents or a guardian."

I gave him a polite smile. "I understand."

As soon as Neala and I walked out of the bank building, I called Med.

"I'm at the First Bank of the Philippines. They need your signature on the account."

"That's fine. I will go there this afternoon and take of it. How's everything coming on our school?"

"A man from the Board of Education came by and stated I must have all personnel on my staff before they will give me my certification as a school."

"I am in need of another teacher. Do you know of anyone who could fill these shoes?"

Med hesitated for a moment. 'Ali, I'm retiring from the hospital at the end of the month.

I would like to help you teach."

"Would you give up your retirement to help me?"

"I would love to teach the students about medicine and I have a great desire for helping people. That is if you would have me as one of your teachers."

I squeezed my phone in my hand. "It would be an honor to have you. The knowledge you have gained over the years of public service is not in any book. You could also teach them about business."

"Med, I have thought about how many students to take on at first. I think that thirty would be enough to start off with. And I am also going to open the school to any student who wants to learn. There are a lot of students in the outlying areas of the province that would like to have the opportunity to go to school."

Med didn't say a word. He paused for several seconds. "I like it. If we can teach these students and have them become a productive person, it would be worth it."

"Here's a list of personnel that we will need to hire to open the school. We're in need of a student counselor, caretakers, chefs, maintenance personal, office staff, and of course, teachers.

You have filled in one of those positions."

"Okay, here's what I would do. Go on different social media sites and advertise what you are wanting. Then, I would put up flyers at different locations where lots of people will see them. You will also need to find out what the salaries are for these different vocations. You may even go over to the college and put up some flyers there as well. Some students are in need of an internship in order to graduate."

"Thanks," I said. "I'll check at the college first."

Once we got into Neala's SUV, she looked at me. "Are we getting ahead of ourselves again?"

I gave her a dumb look. "Say what?"

Then it hit me. There won't be a bank account without one of my parent's signatures on the account.

I called my father. 'I'm in need of a parent signature at the bank in order to setup an account for the school. Are you or momma available to come here and meet me?"

"Hold on for a moment and let me check."

'I can be there in an hour. Is that okay?"

"That's fantastic," I said.

Sitting in Neala's car listening to her style of music, we made small talk about the weather, volcanoes, and nothing in particular. I caught sight of my father's SUV pulling up next to where we were parked.

As we were finishing up with the account information, Dr. Montoya walked into the bank.

"Ali, I'm glad to see you."

My father recognized the doctor. "Hello, Med."

"Hello, Francis."

"I see that you and Ali are on a joint account for the new school."

"Why yes. I have to have access if I need to add any additional funds."

My father raised an eyebrow. "Do you think this school will ever make any money?"

"Not at first. But in time, if the student's grades show a great improvement, then getting outside funding is possible. You know as well as I do that all projects must start from the ground up in order to grow."

My father seemed hesitant. "Ali, I will see you at home tonight."

"Med, I'm going over to the college to talk to the dean. Care to come along?"

"I would like that. I haven't been to a school in a lot of years."

Med, Neala and myself headed over to Zamora College. As soon as we entered the school, I got the same questions asked about me as before by the students in the hallway. "What's that little girl doing here?"

Med caught the stares. "Do you always get this kind of welcome?"

"Pretty much. It blows their mind when they find out that I'm a teacher."

"I bet it does. If I were a student again, I know it would shock me."

Both of us walked into the main office with a smile and pride in our step.

"Hello Ms. Cruz. And who did you bring with you today?"

"This is Dr. Montoya. We need to speak with the Dean, Mrs. Bautista."

The secretary called the dean's extension. Two minutes later, she walked in to where we were standing.

"Hello Ali. How are you today?"

"I'm fine. This is Dr. Montoya."

"Are you wanting to setup another class here?"

"No, I think that I am better suited to teach in my own

school. Dr. Montoya bought a building that we are converting into a school named ASHE, which stands for Advanced Studies of Higher Education.

"I see. So where is this school going to be located?"

"It's on the north side of Legaspi City. It used to be the Seafarer Hotel."

"I know that place. I didn't know that it was up for sale."

Med spoke up. "I purchased the hotel buildings a few days ago. We are going to start up a school that will be the envy of all colleges and universities."

"Mrs. Bautista, why we came here is to see if any of your students would like to work full or part time. We are in need of a counselor, cooks, maintenance personnel, and office staff. I will make sure that their pay is equivalent or better than most positions."

"I don't know of anyone right off hand, but I can put a flyer up advertising your job postings."

"Thanks. That would be great. They can call me or stop by to see if the positions have been filled."

The following morning, Neala and I watched a group of workers installing several blackboards in the different classrooms.

While they were completing their task, Neala and I overheard voices coming down the hallway. She went into guard mode. Looking around the corner of the door opening, I caught sight of eight students that I had in my class at Zamora College.

"Good morning," I said as they approached.

"Hey Ali. It's good to see you again," Henry said.

"What are you guys up to?"

"We heard you were looking for help to open your school."

"As you can see, my school is not ready to be opened as of yet. I still haven't been certified by the Board of Education. We are still putting everything together. Do you know of anyone who can cook, do housecleaning, and building maintenance? I am also in need of a secretary who can do office work. Without these positions filled, I cannot open. I will also need a certified counselor for the students."

One of the girls who had left my class was standing with Henry. She gave me a strange look.

"I didn't think that you were for real. That's why I left your class. I found out later that everyone who stayed in your class, aced the test they took. I'm in need of your teachings. I want to be a teacher someday and go back to my village to teach the students there who cannot go to school."

I smiled at her. "That is why I have decided to open this school. I want to teach as many students as possible. Dr. Montoya and I have agreed that it would be a wonderful thing to help our country."

"I'm sorry, but I don't recall your name."

"My name is Alexa Rivera."

Henry raised an eyebrow. "Ali, what happened to you that day you walked out of the classroom?"

I stayed quiet for several seconds. "When Neala didn't return from the restroom, I went looking for her. I found her lying on the restroom floor. Someone hit me from behind with a stun gun. A drug lord had his gang kidnap me. Under gunpoint, I was forced to make a drug for them. I also found out that they had taken my little sister as hostage. Neala came to my rescue and was able to eliminate the drug lord and his gang but, they killed my little sister. That was a heavy price to pay for having my gift. My mind was no longer coherent. I prayed to our Lord to help me find the strength to carry on. I am here today because he believes in me and what I can do for the people of our country."

Alexa stood next to me. "I'm sorry I doubted you. If we can find you the people who can do the jobs that you are needing, will you teach us?"

"What grades are you in as of this last semester?"

Henry looked at me. "We have all graduated from Zamora."

"I need to know what each of you are going to do next. Let's go sit down and discuss your future."

Three of them are wanting to become doctors. "You three will need to see Dr. Montoya. He is the Chief Surgeon at Memorial Hospital. He is going to retire his position there at the end of the month and is going to teach all the sciences that deal with medicine. He comes with an impeccable record of achievements while he worked at the hospital."

"Alexa, you have already told me what you want to do. How about the other four?"

Each one spoke up. "We want to work in the business world: accounting, office management, sales, etc."

"I'm in need of your services here. If you would like to work here while you are studying, I will pay you a good wage for your services."

Dr. Montoya heard me speaking to the students. As he stepped into the room that we occupied, I introduced him to everyone in the group.

"Med, we have three students who are looking to expand their knowledge into the medical field. All eight were in my class when I was teaching at Zamora. They all have graduated and are looking to expand their knowledge. There are also four here who received a business degree and are looking for work and more education. Alexa here wants to be a teacher and go back to her village and teach the students there."

Med smiled. "That's excellent. That will leave us with finding maintenance personnel as well as three cooks, and one or two counselors."

Henry sat up in his chair. "I will talk to my brother. He used to do maintenance for a hotel in Legaspi. He is working in a warehouse now, but it doesn't hurt to ask."

Med focused on him. "You're right. Check with him. We

pay a good wage to have people working for us. Or he may know of someone who can fill the positions that we still need."

I got into the conversation. "If you want to work for us, we will need you to fill out some paperwork. Afterwards, we need to get computers and any office furniture that you may need."

While they were filling out paperwork, Med and I discussed what was inessential for the students. "We are in need of computer desks, chairs, and anything that will bring this school to life." Neala started making notes on her phone tablet.

"Med, we will also need some sort of transportation for the students. The size will be determined on how many students we have."

"Ali, I've been thinking about that. We need to limit ourselves to no more than twenty students to start off with. We can always expand after we get our feet wet."

"We have four here already that want to take their education to the next level. Adding eight more would not be a problem. With a total of twelve, we could keep our budget down some by you and I doing the teaching instead of hiring anyone else. And we also have one of the students here already who wants to be a teacher. She could help in her area of expertise."

Med thought for a moment. "I like it. Let's pull everyone together so we could have a discussion."

With everyone gathered in the lobby area, I stood up. "Okay everyone. Here is what Med and I have decided to do with this school. As soon as we have the proper staff on our payroll, and we have our certification from the Board of Education, we want Alexa to help here with teaching. This will give her some experience. The four of you that have a BS in business can help run this school. And the other three who want to work in the medical field will be working with Dr. Med Montoya. He has connections with other doctors and will be a great inspiration for you. We don't have any books to work from yet, so I guess

I'll put different subjects on the board. I will be pushing your knowledge to its limits. I teach in an unusual way, but my results are top notch. There is no time limit on your studies. If you want to stay here or travel to and from your home, that is up to you. Now for this first class, we are not going to charge any of you tuition fees. Everything will be free for now. As you can see, Med and I are starting this school from the ground up. We had nothing to work with except the devotion to teach students who have a desire to excel in their education. Okay, let's not take this topic any further. Do any of you still have any schoolbooks?"

All the students raised their hands.

"Great. Can you bring them with you tomorrow? I would like to see what subjects you have been studying and what books I need to buy. Also, one more thing I just thought of, since there are only eight students to start with, I will give you my cell phone number and I would like to have yours as well. I would like one person to take charge of getting any information to the group. Henry, would you be that person? Someone I can count on?"

At first, he seemed a little hesitant. Then he smiled. "I would like that."

"Then it's settled. I'm giving you a set of keys to the main gate and building. I live in Bacacay with my parents. Since most of you live in the Legaspi area, you are a lot closer to the school. As you are well aware that sometimes things happen. Storms, volcano eruptions, etc. I may not be able to get here as soon as you. If we work together, then we can be a team and take this school to the next level." Everyone liked what I was saying.

"The task of getting this school started is a daunting one to say the least. Med and I have a lot to accomplish. We are going to go and buy new computers, desks, and anything else that we may need. If you can think of anything, please give me a call. Oh, and I almost forgot. Pulling up the list of things on my cell phone, we are in need of a land-line phone system and internet service.

I will take care of this problem myself right now." After several minutes with the spokesperson in their accounting department, I had a schedule for the service to be hooked up. "Now I have one less problem to take care of."

"Okay everyone, if you would like to leave now, that's okay with me. We will start tomorrow. Hopefully, I'll have the computers here and get the internet hooked up."

After everyone had left, I placed a call to the company for internet service.

# ~Chapter Ten~

Med, can we go and buy some furniture, and computers? Any school desks that we may need, I can order online at a school supply warehouse."

"Oh sure. We are going to have to have them anyway."

Neala sat across from me listening to our conversation. Studying the screen on her cell phone. "The Computer Store here in Legaspi has computers on sell this week. We can also check in Bacacay where we bought our last office desks to see if they are still in business."

"That sounds like a plan to me."

Med smiled. "We do need to go shopping, don't we?"

The three of us piled into Med's SUV. Since I'm the youngest of this group, I let the grown-ups sit up front, sort of speaking. Looking at my cell phone, my mind was going through the paces that we took when my first company started up.

"Med, we will also need to check on some kitchen appliances. Since the first students do not want to stay there, then I see no reason other than having a microwave oven. There's a gas stove in the kitchen that should be usable. We'll also need to check on the refrigerator to be sure that it still works. We will also need to have the place sprayed for bugs. And have a land-line phone system installed. Then we will need to have the water turned on so the restrooms will work. Plus, we will need several printers for the computers."

"Neala, am I missing anything?" She thought for a moment. "We also need to have a storm shelter built so we don't have to leave the premises if we get caught in a storm."

"That's a good idea," I said.

"Med, can you think of anything?"

Med scratched his black and grey beard. "We'll need textbooks for different sciences, mathematics, history, and languages. That's the main ones that I can think of right now."

"I'll look into it," making a note in my phone. A thought came to mind. Opening up AMN Industries was nothing compared to opening a school from scratch.

Pulling into the driveway of The Computer Store, the three of us made our way towards the desktop computers. A saleswoman strolled over to where Med and Neala were standing.

"May I help you folks with a computer?" I stood back and watched this scenario unfold.

Med studied this young woman. "We are in need of twelve desktop models. And we need two high speed printers".

I watched this saleswoman choke on Med's words. I saw the expression on Neala's face. It was priceless. The saleswoman recomposed herself like a professional. "Did you say twelve computers and two printers?"

Med smiled. "I did."

She moved us towards her top-of-the-line models.

"Where are the ones that you advertised this week?" I asked.

She pointed towards them. "They are basic models. They have slow processors and little memory. Can you show us the middle range models?" This salesperson seemed a little perturbed that a little girl such as me would be asking about the middle models and not the high-end units. A sale of twelve high end models would make her Salesperson-Of-The-Year. Med drifted back towards the middle units. "How many of these do you have?"

"Let me check." She left for a few minutes so she could check the inventory.

Returning back to us with a wide smile on her face.

"We have nineteen of these units in stock."

Med looked at her. "I want twelve of them."

I could tell that this saleswoman just made her quota for the month and then some.

"Now for printers. We have these models," she said. Looking them over, Med chose two laser models. After the bill was paid, the saleswoman couldn't stop saying thank you enough.

Neala chimed in. "I bet she just made salesperson of the month here."

Med didn't say a thing. I looked at Neala. "I know that's right. Now we can go over to where we purchased our desks before." Making our way towards Bacacay, I caught sight of Neala's sixth sense kicking in. From her side of the car, she couldn't see the Mayon very well. She turned in her seat in every direction possible so she could watch our surroundings. I knew something wasn't right. Watching her body movements, "Neala, are you okay?" I asked.

"Not sure. Something's not right." Med didn't know what we were talking about. Then we felt a tremor as the ground shook beneath Med's SUV.

Neala looked at me. "I think the Mayon is waking up again." Then the earth shook harder. Med hit the brakes to slow down our forward motion. Rolling down the windows so we could see the road, the three of us stuck our heads out looking for any crevices in the road. As the noise surrounding us became even louder, I raised my voice. "We don't need to drive into one of these crevices." Med slowed down even more as we continued to move forward. The people who were walking on the side of the road had a terrified look on their faces. I could tell that panic was setting in.

Then the earth under us went calm. The three of us watched all sides of the road and the hillside. We hadn't gone maybe five more kilometers when the earth next to the right side of our car just fell off. I watched several trikes and a small group of people just vanish as they fell into this fiery pit. Their screams were horrific as they cried for help. Med stopped his SUV. Covering our faces with our hands, we ran over to see if there was anything that we could do to save them. We moved as close to the edge of the drop-off as possible. With our watery eyes and coughing from the sulphur smell, we tried covering our faces with our shirt tail but standing there for any length of time was not possible. The heat permeating from the molten lava was unbearable. The only thing left of the people that I could see were just a few pieces of clothing burning into an ash.

Staring at the roadway, I conceded that part of the asphalt road was taken away. The drop-off started on the edge of the road and looked to be at least one-hundred meters down. I stood mesmerized watching the lava flow heading away from us as it found the least resistant path towards the ocean.

Reality kicked in. I had just witnessed no less than twenty people disappear. I started crying. Seeing these people just vanish was horrifying. Neala began yelling over the noise coming from the earth within. "We have got to leave here. Now! It's not safe to stay here." I knew she was right. There was nothing that any of us could do to help them.

Returning to Med's SUV, we headed away from the carnage. We hadn't gone just a couple more kilometers when there was a loud explosion in front of us. "What was that?" I screamed. The black smoke and ash were so thick, we could not see the road. Med slowed his SUV to a snail's pace. After what we had just witnessed, I didn't want to end up with the same fate. I closed my eyes and said a prayer. Neala and Med heard me. After I was done, they chimed, "Amen."

Med looked into his rear-view mirror at me. "I hope he heard you. We need his mighty hand about right now. I have no idea what is in front of us or behind us. I don't mind saying that I'm terrified right now." Neala saw the facial expression on the doctor's face.

"Med, stop your car. Let me drive."

"Okay," was the only thing Med said. Neala and I noticed Med's hands were starting to shake. He stopped the car and put it into park. Neala jumped and ran around to the driver's side. After the switch was made, Neala proceeded to move us forward again. I knew that she had nerves of steel but moving in a blackout situation put her at the top of my list as one of the baddest of the bad.

Watching Med and his body movements, he put his hands under his armpits. He was trying to stop them from shaking. It hit me as to why Med stopped being a surgeon. He has a medical condition that has started to cause his hands to shake. He turned and looked at me sitting in the back seat. He knew that I now know of his condition. I didn't say a word. As Neala continued moving us forward, I held onto the cross that Father Bayon had given me before I left for Switzerland. Within the hour, we moved only two more kilometers through all of the smoke and haze. As we continued our forward movement, we could see the air was now becoming less dense. Neala pushed on. Another five minutes of our lives had passed when we could finally see blue skies again. Neala picked up speed for several more kilometers. Finding the first place where she could park, we stopped. I didn't see it at first because my eyes were redden from all of the volcanic smoke but I could hear what sounded like water running down the side of a mountain. Neala and Med also heard what had caught my attention. The three of us made our way over to this beautiful cascade of nature's most precious gift. Cupping a hand full, I did a smell test looking for any sulphur, then a taste test. It was clean and fresh. The three of us must have stayed by the stream for close to an hour resting. Looking at Neala's and Med's face, the three of us must have looked like zombies out of a horror movie. Our eyes were a deep shade of red with tears that wouldn't stop flowing and our skin was covered in a pale grey shade of ash.

Neala sat up from where she was lying down. "Come on. We have to be going." Med looked at me. "Ali, I think our dear Lord heard your prayer."

I stayed silent for several seconds. "I believe you're right," I said. I knelt down next to the stream and bowed my head. I thanked him for saving us and providing us with this water to drink.

I know that death is a cruel brother to life and there is no arguing or debating it. When the time comes for us to leave this life, we will not be able to stop it. That's just the way it is.

Pulling up to the front of my house, my parents and Minda ran out to greet us. They saw Med's SUV covered in ash. My mother was sobbing.

"We thought we lost you. The news reports stated that the Mayon had erupted towards Legaspi."

"It did momma. We were heading back here to check on some office desks when we got caught in the smoke and ash cloud. We couldn't see very far. It made traversing the road dangerous. My mother and father gave me a hug. The sulphur smell from our clothes told the whole story. Minda turned a lip upwards. She wanted to mess with me for a moment. She backed up putting her hands on her hips. She looked me up and down with some serious eye movement.

"What did I tell you about playing with fire around a volcano?" She wiggled her finger at me. "You're going to have to scrub yourself with a cement brush. And your clothes."

Then she giggled at me. I gave her my evil eye. Then we smiled at each other and giggled like the young girls we still are.

I needed some laughter right now. The adults knew that Minda and I liked to joke around. We were as close to being biological sisters as humanly as possible.

Med and Neala walked back to Med's SUV.

Med stopped for a moment before getting into his car. "Ali, we'll talk some more in a few days."

Neala smiled. "Ali, I will be back later. I'm going to get cleaned up."

"I know that's right. I hear a shower calling my name as well."

For the next few days after staring at death, Neala and I sat in her SUV making small talk about this or that. A brain wave hit me. "We never bought any desks. Are you up to checking out the no-name furniture store?"

Neala turned and smiled at me. "Sure." She started her car and we headed over to see if the small furniture store was still in business.

Pulling into the empty parking lot, I could just make out a name on the side of the dirty building. "Juan's Furniture."

Neala and I made our way to the front door of the establishment. Finding the door locked, I peered through the glass door. "The place is full of furniture," I said. I rang the buzzer. After about a minute, Neala and I turned to leave when I heard the door unlock. An older woman appeared. "May I help you?" she asked.

"Are you still selling furniture?" I asked.

"Yes and no. What I mean is we are not in business any longer. Since my husband passed away last year. I can't keep up with the business anymore at my age. We still have lots of furniture that I need to get rid of. Is there anything that you are particularly looking for?"

"We are in need of office desks and chairs," I said.

"How many do you need?" she asked.

"We will need ten of each."

"Let's go and look at what we have left."

Entering the office area of her building, she took us to where all the office desks were kept. I counted eleven.

"I will take these ten desks and these chairs." Standing there looking at the surrounding furniture, an idea hit me. Instead of buying individual student desks, we can put in large tables and chairs for the students. Just like I used in Switzerland.

"Do you have any large tables? Six to be exact," I said.

She thought for a moment. "Let's go over there," pointing a finger towards another wall. There were several stacks of two-meter tables leaning against the wall. "I'll take six of these and twelve chairs."

Neala looked at what I wanted to buy. "I think that just about covers it," she said.

The woman looked at Neala.

"Is there anything else that you need, my dear?" she asked.

Neala just smiled pointing a finger at me. "She's the one who needs the furniture." This woman looked puzzled. A young child wanting to buy so much furniture.

"I studied the woman's face. "What's your name Mam?"

"It's Mrs. Dominguez. My husband was Juan Dominguez."

"I have dealt with your husband before. I bought office furniture from him about four years ago."

"I remember him saying that a very young girl bought a lot of furniture then."

"I was five at that time. Now, I'm nine."

She studied me for several seconds. "How do you wish to pay for this?" she asked.

"Do you still take plastic?" I said.

"I do. I haven't shut down the business account yet."

"Great. I will need to have it delivered to this address."

"I know this place. It's the Seafare Hotel."

"It used to be. Now it is going to be a school. I know it may take a few days before you are able to deliver everything. The road to Legaspi may be damaged from the Mayon volcano erupting. Here is my cell number if there is going to be a problem with delivery."

"Thanks, dear. I'll tell my driver, and I'll get back with you if he has any problems on making the delivery."

"Thank you," I said.

# ~Chapter Eleven~

Early the next morning, my mind was in full swing. I placed a call. "Henry, its Ali. Are you okay?" I asked.

"I'm fine."

"Have you checked with the rest of the group?"

"I have talked to everyone except Alexa. I haven't been able to get in touch with her. She is staying with her grandparents while she's attending school. I'll keep trying and let you know."

"Can you go and check out the school buildings? I'm not sure if the road is open going through Legaspi from here. I know parts are damaged from the Mayon erupting several days ago."

"I will check it out and get back with you when I find out any information."

"Okay, thanks," I said.

I tried calling Alexa, but I got the same information as Henry.

My father watched me as I was in business mode. After several more calls, I sat down at the dining table.

"Want a cup of coffee?" he asked.

"That's sounds wonderful," I said.

He saw the look of discontentment on my face.

"Is there anything I can do to help?"

"I cannot get in touch with one of the students. She's not answering her phone. Also, the road to Legaspi may be damaged. I saw the edge of it fall off into a crevice when we were trying to get home."

My father handed me my coffee. "I'll check into it. I know a few people who may have some answers."

After about a half an hour, my father hung up his phone. "I just had a conversation with the Corps of Engineers head man. He says the road from here is closed. They are assessing the damage and they're not sure how long it'll before the road will be open again."

"Thanks dad, for checking on that for me."

I placed a call to Henry. "I just found out the road is closed and there is no answer as to when it will be reopened. I guess the only way to Legaspi is around the Mayon. And that will take several hours."

"Please check out the buildings at the school if you can?"

"I already have. The power is off and there is a lot of ash covering about everything in sight. The good news is there doesn't seem to be any broken windows or other damage."

"I guess everything has been put on hold until we can assess what we need to do next. I'll keep in touch."

I called Neala. "I was just informed that Legaspi City and the surrounding area is covered with ash and the main road has been damaged. I called Henry and he checked on the school buildings. Other than being covered in ash, they seem to be okay."

"I'll make some calls to people I know over there."

"Have them get in touch with Henry. He has a set of keys to the gate and the buildings." After giving her his number, she hung up. A call to Med was next on my list.

"Good morning sunshine," he said.

"You're in a good mood," I said.

"I am. I'm grateful to be alive. The good Lord has blessed me with another day of life on this earth."

Pausing for several seconds…"Med you're right. I should be thankful as well. I have let the human side of me take control of my life and the spiritual side slip to the back of my mind. I will say my prayers as soon as I hang up. I've talked to Henry. The school is okay except it is covered in ash. Neala is checking to see if someone will go inside and check it out for us. The road from here is closed. It was damaged and the only way to Legaspi is around the opposite side of the Mayon. I can imagine the traffic going to and from Legaspi will be horrendous."

"Ali, I'll talk to you later. I'm having my car washed as we speak. I'm afraid the ash has done a number to the paint."

After hanging up, a thought occurred to me. Med must have been very close to seeing death. That's why he was shaking so badly when he drove into the ash cloud.

Taking my coffee, I strolled outside and sat down near the pile of leaves that always seems to grow in front of my mother's small store. Minda saw me sitting there with my head bowed down. Sitting down next to me, she didn't say a word. We just sat there for several seconds like that.

"Hey girlfriend, are you okay?" she asked.

"Yeah, I was just praying. I think I need to see Father Bayon. So much is still happening to me. It didn't hit me until I just talked to Med. We were so close to death by driving through that ash cloud. I'm taking everyday life for granted and nothing is going to stop me, not even death. After my conversation with Med, I have neglected my relationship with our Lord and that needs to change."

Getting up, I grabbed the broom from my mother's store. "Those leaves need to be attended to as well," I said.

Minda stood back as I started sweeping. After several minutes of tackling the task at hand, a strong breeze kicked up. Looking up, I saw the leaves moving around in a circle like a whirlwind. Minda looked at me, then at the leaves lying on the ground. She saw the message spelled in the leaves as well. "Yes." Then the breeze started up again and the message disappeared.

"Did you see that?" I asked.

Minda moved her hair away from her eyes. "I did."

I placed another call to Neala. "Could you take me over to see Father Bayon?"

"Sure, I can be there in fifteen minutes."

"Thanks, Neala."

My parents were just finishing up their breakfast when I sat down at the table. "Neala is coming over to get me. I want to go and see Father Bayon."

"Is there anything that I can do?" my father asked.

"No," I said softly. "I need to speak with the Father on some thing that's bothering me."

"I see," my father said. "We'll wait here with you until Neala arrives."

"That's okay," I said. Then reality kicked in. "You're right. I keep forgetting about the world that we live in. Nothing for us is normal anymore."

My father gave me a hug.

Minda stood there watching us.

My father moved next to her and gave her a big hug as well. My mother looked at what was taking place. She pulled us together into a tight group. I noticed my mother had tears in her eyes. She looked into each of our faces. "We're a family and that's all that matters."

With a knock on the front door, our family gathering broke up. Opening the door, Neala could tell that I had been crying. She rested her right hand on her pistol. "Is everything okay?" she asked.

"It is. We were just having a family conversation."

Neala saw the faces of my parents and Minda. They too had red eyes.

"Can we leave now?" I asked.

"Oh sure."

While we were making our way over to the St. Rose of Lima Parish Church, Neala seemed to have a puzzled look on her face.

"Care to talk about why you and your family all have red eyes?"

I stayed silent for several seconds. "I've forgotten my place in this world and have been taking life for granted. After what happened to us yesterday, with the Mayon erupting and talking to Med this morning, I realized that life is very precious. I have let my human side take control and that's bothering me a lot. That's why I must see Father Bayon."

Neala glanced over at me. "I see."

As soon as we stopped in the parking lot of the church, Neala reached over and grabbed my hand. Squeezing my hand gently, she smiled.

Opening the front door, I could see Father Bayon was having a conversation with a young couple and their small boy. Seeing the ambient light in the room glow brighter from the front door being opened, he glanced over at us. Returning his attention to his company, he had them gather around him and they prayed. After they had finished their conversation with the Father, they left.

"Ali, Neala, so good to see you. What brings you here?" he asked.

"Father, I need to speak with you."

Neala sat down in a rear pew while I walked with the Father towards the front of the church. "Father, I'm in need of your spiritual guidance. I seem to have let the human side of me take control of my life, and I have let my spiritual side go to the back of my mind. With so much death happening around me, I'm becoming immune to it. Like it's just the way things are supposed to be. But I know better."

Father Bayon sat silent listening to me speak. "Yes, my

child, you are right. Our Lord is watching and guiding us along our journey in life. What you are witnessing in this life is far from being over. Your travels along the road of human life will show you the good and the bad in the human race. Keep the Lord in your heart. He will help you along your journey."

"Father, may we kneel at the cross?"

Neala got up to stand on my right side. "May I join you?"

"Oh, please do," I said.

Neala's thoughts drifted off for a moment. Life and death are just numbers on a piece of paper to the powers that are controlling the mass populations of the world. They created it and they will destroy it for that power.

Father Bayon began his prayer.

# ~Chapter Twelve~

W here to?" Neala asked as we sat in her SUV. "I would like to see for myself just how much ash is covering our school. The only thing I can think of right now is how to get it cleaned up would be to have a heavy rain. I watched the weather reports, and we are not expecting any rainfall until the end of the week."

Neala glanced at me. "Not sure how long this trip will be, but I'm game. Somewhere along our way, we'll have to stop and fill up the fuel tank."

After buying fuel and several bottles of water, Neala and I were off on another venture. "I have never been around the west side of the Mayon before, so this trip will be something new to me."

Winding our way along narrow roads, we did encounter a lot more traffic as people were coming and going from Legaspi City. In some areas, we had to nearly crawl because of how heavy the traffic was. Neala blew a strand of hair off of her face. "This is like driving in Manila," she stated. She hit the horn, shifted gears and hit the horn again. People were everywhere along the road.

Studying a map I had laid in my lap, "This trip should only take us about an hour. But I'm guessing it's going take us an upwards of at least six. Then we have to make the return trip back home."

Neala looked at me since we were stopped in the middle of an intersection and haven't moved in almost eight minutes.

She studied my reactions as I stared out the window. "Do we continue or turn back?" Looking at the clock on her dash, we've been traveling for almost two hours and haven't gone maybe fifteen kilometers.

"At this rate, we wouldn't make it to the school until night fall. And I'm not so sure if the electricity is on in Legaspi." I needed to make a decision now.

"Let's go back. We wouldn't be able to see any of the school buildings to access what needs to be done. Without any electricity, we won't have any air conditioning, and we would have to breathe the ash-filled air. That would be bad for our health. Until it rains and it helps wash the ash down, I don't want to risk our lives just to get a look at our school buildings."

Neala smiled at me. "Good decision." After turning around, we headed back to Bacacay.

Pulling up to the front of our home, Neala and I made our way inside. Putting our things down, I headed towards the kitchen.

"My parents and Minda should be coming home in about an hour," I said.

"Neala, are you hungry?"

"I'm starving," she replied.

"Okay then, let's see what we can whip up before they come home." I found the ingredients to make Sinigang soup with fish, string beans, and rice.

Neala watched me working in the kitchen trying to put everything together. "Can I help?" she asked.

"That would be great," I said.

I heard the front door opening and I could see Minda making her way towards the kitchen.

"Hey Ali. How's things in your world."

"Okay I guess, considering the mess the Mayon has made for us."

"How's work going?" I asked.

"I was able to close a deal on one-hundred-thousand bags of product today."

"That's great. I always knew you could handle the job." She smiled at me as she went to our bedroom. My parents strolled into the kitchen at a leisurely pace.

"Smells good," my mother said.

"It should be ready in about a half an hour and a half."

My father waited for everyone to clear out of the room and then he gave me a hug.

"I understand that Minda just made a big sale of our product?"

"She did and we'll have to add a few more employees to our payroll."

"That's wonderful. I know there are plenty of people who would like to have a steady job.

My father just smiled at me. "To Tibea. Though I never met her, I wish I could have."

"To Tibea," I replied.

After we enjoyed this delicious meal, my mother began to clean up the dining table.

"I'll do this momma. You go and sit with daddy." She smiled and left. Neala watched me.

"I'll help."

"Thanks," I said.

While Neala and I put the finishing touches to the kitchen, I heard the television weather spokesperson announce, "A low-pressure system is developing about six-hundred kilometers off the coast of the lower area of the Visayas Islands. Reconnaissance aircraft are being sent to check out this area. We'll keep you advised of any development."

I rushed out of the kitchen so I could catch the last part of the weather cast. Sitting on the floor, my mind focused on the satellite image. It was showing a large disturbance off the Province of Eastern Salmar. Locking my eyes onto the television screen, I began to form the calculations in my head. The wind patterns for the next several days, in that area, were going to be crucial as to where this storm was going to hit. Everybody in the room fell silent as they watched my body movements. It was like I had put them in a trance.

"I know where this storm is going," I said.

No one questioned how or why I knew.

My father responded. "What are you going to do?"

"I'm going to call the PAGASA (Philippine Atmospheric, Geophysical and Astronomical Service Administration) and tell them."

After finding their phone number, I made the call.

"The PAGASA Weather Service, may I help you?" the woman asked.

"I need to speak with the person in charge of watching the storm off the Coast of the Visayas Islands."

"One moment please."

"This is Mr. Perez. How may I help you?"

"My name is Ali Cruz, and I know where this storm is going to hit. I also know that this storm will become a typhoon in the next twelve to eighteen hours."

Mr. Perez knew from the sound of my voice that I was a young person. "How old are you and who gave you this information? The reconnaissance aircraft hasn't reported anything to us yet."

"I'm nine-years-old and no one has told me anything. I saw the satellite image on the news a few minutes ago and I know where this storm is heading."

"Little girl, I don't know how or where you are getting your information, but we have highly trained personnel who know about these storms."

"Okay. If you make a call to the President of the Philippines, he will tell you that I'm for real and I know what I'm talking about."

"What's your name?" he asked.

"Ali Cruz."

After I hung up, Neala had a snickering smile on her face. "Wait till he finds out who he was just talking too. You may have just popped his bubble."

Minda let out a soft giggle.

My mother got up from the sofa. "Coffee anyone?" We all said, "yes, please." I heard my mother mumbling something about me, typhoons, and popping a man's bubble.

It took about an hour before my phone rang. It was Mr. Perez.

"At first, I thought you were just someone making a prank call. We get them all the time. But I had a hunch and asked the general manager to make a call to the president's office. He vouched for you and said that I may learn something if I would just listen to you. Would you like to come here to our office and let's have a chat?"

"Where are you located," I asked.

"We are in Queson City."

"How am I going to get there? I live in Bacacay, in the Albay Province. The only airport around this part is in Legaspi City, and it's closed due to the Mayon volcano."

"Okay then. Go over to Naga City Airport and I'll have a plane there waiting for you."

"Okay, great. I will have my bodyguard with me. Her name is Neala."

"You have a bodyguard?"

"Yes, I do. President Datu assigned her to me."

"You know the president personally?"

"I do, and I have him on speed dial.

"Okay then. How long before you can be in Naga City?"

Looking at Neala. "How long is the drive to Naga Airport?"

"About an hour and a half."

"Figure about two hours then. The traffic is slow due to the Mayon."

"Okay. I'll have a plane waiting for you at eight a.m."

"Before hanging up, give me your cell phone number in case there is a delay." After I ended the call, I told the story to everyone about my newest adventure.

Minda was smiling. "Another government trip."

"Neala, a plane will be picking us up at eight a.m. at Naga City Airport."

"Okay, I'll see you at four o'clock in the morning."

I knew better than to question Neala about leaving so early. At three-forty-five, my alarm was banging my ears. Minda said a few words and rolled over in her bed.

"Sorry," I said in a soft voice as I headed out of our bedroom. The coffee pot had just finished brewing when I heard a slight knock on our door. Opening it to Neala, "coffee just finished," I said. Both of us filled our mugs with the hot brew and headed out the door.

# ~Chapter Thirteen~

Sitting in Neala's SUV just outside the fenced-in tarmac, we watched for any aircraft making its final approach to Naga City Airport. A few minutes after eight, a turboprop aircraft taxied away from the main entrance and headed in our direction. I could read the writing painted on its side. PAGASA. "That's for us," I said grabbing my things.

As soon as the engines were shut down, the main door on the aircraft was opened. I strolled over to the security guard who was standing at the tarmac gate. After a brief conversation, and showing him our passports, he studied our faces to make sure we matched the passport photos. After he was satisfied, he let us pass through the gate. A tall slender man exited the aircraft and made his way towards us.

Neala and I were standing next to the security guard when he stopped in front of me.

"Are you Ali Cruz?" he asked.

"I am and this is Neala."

After taking a few steps towards the aircraft, I turned to face the security guard.

"Thanks," I said.

He smiled. "Have a safe flight."

The government employee held out his hand. "Hello. My name is Francisco De Leon. I will be escorting you to our office." After leaving Naga City Airport, Neala and I sat quietly in our seats. I studied the land masses that were passing below us while Neala kept full attention on Mr. De Leon and the flight crew. Everything seemed okay to Neala, but she was not going to let her guard down.

As soon as we landed, we were escorted to a waiting car.

Sitting quietly, Neala and I watched our surroundings as we passed the general population going about their business. Another peaceful ride to a place I have never been. Studying the street signs as we passed them, I made a mental note to myself just in case we needed to return to the airport. I got a reassuring feeling from Neala when she grasped my hand and squeezed it gently.

I looked up at her face and smiled. "This should be interesting," I said in a faint voice. She smiled back. "It should indeed."

As soon as we entered the building, we had to go through another security check. Neala was told to leave her weapon with the guard at this point. She didn't like it, but there was nothing that she could do to change their minds. After passing security, we were led to Mr. Perez's office by an older woman with short grayish hair who didn't smile. With a light knock on Mr. Perez's office door, she opened it. "Please take a seat. Mr. Perez will be with you in a moment." Several minutes later, Mr. Perez entered his office. Seeing me and Neala sitting there, he smiled as he sat behind his desk.

"So, Ali, how do you know about these storms? What education do you have to predict what a storm can or will do?"

"Well for starters, I have more diploma's than you have wall space. I have the highest IQ of any person in the country and perhaps the world. Do I need to go on?"

"No, that won't be necessary."

"I know about these storms because I study them. I want to know where they're going and what damage it will cause.

Especially when it comes to human life. I also started a company called AMN Industries and invented a product that makes concrete almost indestructible."

"I have heard about your company. It's growing at an enormous rate."

"It is. We now have over two-hundred employees and eight offices throughout the Philippines. Now about this particular storm that formed two days ago. What are the latest developments?"

"Follow me and I'll take you to where we watch the weather here in our country as well as the world."

After we entered a secured room, there were dozens of computers monitors along the walls with at least ten people watching the weather patterns from around the world.

Mr. Perez pointed at a monitor that was centered on the wall. "The storm that developed off the Coast of Visayas has been given the name of Basil. So far it's only a small cyclone."

"May I see the latest satellite images?"

I was led over to a computer screen that showed a satellite view of the Philippines. "Can you zoom in on that storm?" I asked.

He zoomed the image on the screen to twenty-five percent. "Okay, what are the current winds speeds and direction? What is the current water temperature where the storm is sitting at and where are the high and low-pressure areas at this moment?" I studied everything that I asked for and then I went around and studied each computer monitor on the wall.

Mr. Perez pointed at a particular monitor. "The computer model out of Japan is what we normally use for the storms here in the Philippines."

After I made my observations, I looked at Mr. Perez. "At this time of year, the wind currents in the upper atmosphere are going to stall here." I pointed my finger at a map of the Visayas Islands. "A high-pressure cell will move in here and cause the low pressure to pull the storm into the Northern Salmar Province. This stalling effect will turn this storm into a typhoon."

Everyone in the room fell quiet as I told them what I thought this storm was going to do.

A couple of the employees whispered. "Who is she and how does she know so much about predicting what the weather will do? Especially since she's only a small child."

Mr. Perez asked everyone to quiet down for a moment. "This is Ali Cruz. Some of you may have heard of her". One young lady spoke up. "I have. I was in a science class at the University of the Philippines when she was asked to solve a complex math problem. She answered it in less than fifteen seconds. Our instructor had never seen anything like it before. Then she put a problem on the board that none of us could answer."

I focused my attention on this person. "That problem I put up was unsolvable," I said. "Everyone in that classroom laughed at me for being just a child so I laughed back."

The young woman smiled. "You did at that."

Mr. Perez spoke up. "Ali has predicted that the storm now called Basil will come ashore along the upper coast of Northern Salmar."

"Ali, what do you think the time-frame is before it moves on land?"

"Given everything that I see here, I would put it at thirty to thirty-six hours before landfall."

"Okay everyone. We have been challenged by a nine-year-old girl. Form a team. Pull all your information together. With everything that you have in front of your right now, what are your predictions for this storm?" Everyone got up and formed a circle. After they looked at each other's notes, the young lady that had spoken as few minutes ago pushed her glasses up. "We believe that this storm will move along the coastline and turn away and head out eastward into the pacific."

"Ali, do you want to change your answer?" Mr. Perez asked.

"No, I'm good. Please do not wait to tell the people that live along the coastline and the towns in the Northern Salmar to prepare for a typhoon."

Mr. Perez smiled. "We got it."

"Okay then. Neala and I will start heading back. I'll watch the news to see what new developments happen."

"Mr. Perez, could you arrange for us transportation back to the airport?"

"I sure can."

Mr. Perez made a call to De Leon to take us back to Naga City Airport.

We thanked him and left. The car ride and the plane ride back to Naga was quiet. As soon as we landed, Neala headed off to retrieve her SUV. We still had an hour or so to drive back home.

*****

Pulling up behind my parent's vehicle, we made our way inside. Seeing everyone was home, I gave each person a hug.

Neala looked at the scene before her. "Ali, I have some things to take care of."

"I'm good," I said.

She smiled and left.

"I'm starving. We didn't eat today. We were so busy at the weather station, I totally forgot about it."

My mother dove into the kitchen cabinets looking for something to cook. "Get cleaned up. I'll have something prepared shortly."

"Okay momma."

My father turned to face me from the sofa. "Ali, how did it go today with the weather folks?"

"Okay, I guess. They didn't seem to like that a young person, such as myself, knew more about this storm than they did. At least that was my take on the outcome. If I'm wrong then they can say that I don't know what I'm talking about, but if I'm right, they'll end up with egg on their faces. We'll just have to wait and see what the next thirty or so hours bring." I overheard my mother mumbling about how her nine-year-old daughter telling a group of meteorologists that she knows more than they do with their own computers.

Minda, my father, and I sat in silence for a moment waiting for the news to come on. The news spokesperson began his announcements. *"Cyclone Basil has just been upgraded by the PAGASA to a typhoon. For the last six hours, it has slowed down as it heads along the coastline of Visayas Islands. Early models indicate that it may turn towards the west along the Northern Salmar Province."*

"That's what I told the director. It looks like he may just have egg on his face by tomorrow."

Minda giggled. "My sister just made the top weather people in the country look bad."

Putting my head down, I rubbed my hands together. "That was not my intentions to put someone or a group of people down. If this storm does what I think that it will do, then I'll call Mr. Perez and apologize."

My father reached for my hand. He squeezed it gently. "What were your intentions for going to their office?"

"I'm not sure. But they believed that this storm was going to turn east and head out to sea. Now they can have the people along its path begin to take shelter. It may just save someone's life."

My father smiled at me. "Good answer. If we can save just one life, then it was worth making this trip. And if you are correct, they will be contacting you to see if you can teach them so they can be better prepared for the next one."

# ~Chapter Forteen~

The next morning just as I was getting out of the shower, I heard a knock on our door. Wrapped in towels like a mummy, I yelled, "Who is it?"

"Neala."

Opening the door for her, she stood there in front of me smiling.

"What's up?" I asked.

"Oh, nothing much. How's your world starting this morning?"

"Okay, I guess. I thought about going back to Zamora and see Mrs. Bautista. I cannot teach sitting here at home."

"Okay, I'm game."

*****

Walking into the main building, I saw several students roaming the halls.

Neala looked at me. "I thought classes don't start until next month."

"I thought so too." We entered the administration office. "Is Mrs. Bautista in her office?" I asked the lady at the front desk.

"She is. Oh Ali, I just realized that it was you. Let me check for you."

After a short conversation, Mrs. Bautista opened her office door.

'Ali, it's good to see you again. How can I help you?"

"The main road down to Legaspi was damaged by the Mayon and I cannot get my new school opened for quite some time. I would like to teach a few students to see if I can help them."

Mrs. Bautista smiled. "Your old classroom is still available. But just like before, you would not be on the payroll of the school so you would not get a paycheck."

"I know. I'm well taken care of. The money is not what I'm after. I want to try to help a few students to start with. If they can excel in their grades, then it will be worth the effort."

"There aren't any classes starting until about five weeks from now. How are you going to get any students to participate in your class?"

"I'm not sure. I did see some students wondering the hall as I came in."

"They're freshman. There is an orientation today for the new students." Just then, Mrs. Bautista's face lit up, "Ali, follow me."

Neala and I walked along side of Mrs. Baustista. Once we entered the auditorium, she looked at me. "Wait here. I need to speak to Mr. Castro for a moment."

Neala looked at me. "Wait till he hears about you. Now this ought to be good."

Mr. Castro raised an eyebrow.

Neala just smiled. "Wait for it."

Mr. Castro raised both arms up. "She's here? Now?"

Mrs. Baustista waved for me to come on stage.

Mr. Castro looked down at me and shook my hand. "I have always wanted to meet you in person. I have heard many stories. You know, some are just too good to be believable."

"I know what you mean," I said.

"Everyone. We have a celebrity among us today. Her name is Ali Cruz. She is nine-years-old and considered by the world to be one of the smartest humans on the planet."

Mr. Castro lowered the microphone for me. I could hear some of the students laughing. "Why I came here today was to find out if I could teach some of you or all of you how to become better students. The Dean, Mrs. Baustista, has given me a small classroom just off the main hallway. I know that the school semester is about to start in a few weeks. My class would be after school for an hour or so each day."

A male student stood up. "How do we know that you can teach us any better than the teachers that work here?"

"The way that I teach has had a proven effect. My best friend, who is now ten-years-old, is the CEO of a company I started four years ago called AMN Industries. My friend's name is Minda Torres. She has a bachelor's degree from the University of the Philippines. She acquired it at the age of nine. Minda and I took the Battle of the Minds contest here at this school and she moved onto the national level."

Another female student asked. "Tell us about you. Why are you teaching instead of making millions of dollars out doing what you started?"

I paused for a moment. 'At the age of four, I discovered that I could read any book. Father Bayon found out about me and my knowledge was tested at every grade level. I was given the gift of knowledge from our Lord and Savior Jesus Christ. I began to put that knowledge to use by helping our community and our country. I invented a product that builds a stronger structure to withstand a super typhoon. But deep down inside of me, I knew that there was more for me to give to the community. Then I knew what my gift was to be used for. That was to teach. I began to use my knowledge to teach my best friend Minda. Now I want to try to help you if I can."

Mr. Castro's mouth seemed to drop open. "So, the rumors are true."

"They are," I said.

"So how many of you would like to take a short course until the regular school starts?" I saw everyone raise their hands. There was close to one-hundred students here. Mrs. Baustista had an amazed look on her face. "I don't think your classroom would hold everyone. We will have to meet here in the auditorium until I can find a larger classroom."

Mr. Castro stood next to me. "If you need any help, I would like to work with you."

"I would like that," I said.

Mrs. Baustista jotted down notes. 'How long will you classes be?" she asked.

"As long as we can have the room."

"You can use this room for the next five weeks. Then we'll have to see what we can do."

Returning my gaze at the students. "Okay everyone. I was given permission to use this room for the next five weeks. Our class can start at eight each morning until five p.m. There will be a lot of subjects to cover and since you do not have any books yet, we'll have to work on things that I put on the board. Since you are a freshman, you will be taking the basic classes of english, math, sciences, to name a few. Are you ready to get started?" Everyone yelled, "Let's do it." Mrs. Baustista left to retrieve a portable blackboard.

"Mr. Castro, we are in need of paper and something to write with."

"I'll see what I can do."

"While the blackboard and something to write on is being looked into, can we start by you telling me your name and what are you wanting to get out of going to college?"

It took nearly an hour to hear each student.

Mrs. Baustista had a blackboard put on stage. "Ali, this orientation was supposed to last for one hour. Some of these students may have to leave."

"I guess I muddied up the water a bit. Sorry"

"Okay everyone. Some of you may have to leave. This orientation was only supposed to last for one hour. Therefore, if you want to start tomorrow, then we can begin then."

Everyone was in agreement. Tomorrow would be better. All of the student body left the room.

"I'm sorry Mr. Castro for interrupting you. I didn't intend to mess up your orientation of the freshman class. I apologize for stepping in."

"No apologies needed. I have already told them about the basics of college life and the things that they will need to know before you arrived. I think this group will surprise a lot of people in this school with their grades after taking your class."

"I hope so."

Neala stayed quiet the whole time. I had forgotten that she was here. She just seemed to just blend into the background. I think that it's best for me if they don't know who she is.

I told my parents and Minda what I did today. At first, the look I got was normal. I heard my mother mumbling as she headed to the kitchen. "That don't surprise me. Take over a class of a hundred students, that's about right for my Ali."

Minda on the other hand got a kick out of me. "Walk into a college and take over a freshman class." she blared out. "How cool. Can I help?"

"Maybe, if you are caught up on your job assignments."

"I am right now. I can come in an hour or so tomorrow morning with you."

"Then would you like to join me for the first hour of class?"

"I sure would," Minda replied.

That night I couldn't sleep. My mind was full of ideas on what to teach the students without any books. This should be an interesting day to say the least.

*****

Seven-thirty in the morning, Neala, Minda, and I were standing on the stage waiting for the students to start wondering in. Looking at my watch, I caught site of the first students arriving. At ten after eight, they were still marching in the door. Mrs. Baustista told me that this auditorium will hold about two-hundred people, and it was nearly full.

Minda looked at me. "What gives?"

I shrugged my shoulders. "Don't know."

The Dean, Mrs. Baustista walked in and I could see her facial expression. She then looked at me. Walking onto the stage, she hesitated for a moment. "What's up?"

"I don't know," I said. "We're shocked to see so many students as well."

Mrs. Baustista turned on the microphone. "In case any of you are wondering about the look we have on our faces; well, we are wondering how the freshman body grew twice in size overnight?" A female student stood up. "A lot of us called our friends from high school. As soon as we mentioned Ali's name, they wanted to sit in on her class. She is legendary among the educational system in our province. I don't doubt that she is very well known though out the country or the world."

Mrs. Baustista smiled. "Then I don't need any introductions."

"Ali, would you like to start your class."

"Thanks Mrs. Baustista."

"Good morning everyone. My name is Ali Cruz. And this person standing next to me is my best friend Minda Torres. She is ten-years-old, and I am nine years of age. After teaching Minda, she passed her high school exit test at the age of six. She now has a bachelor's degree from the University of the Philippines. My younger sister who is no longer with us, was only five and could read at a twelfth-grade level."

Minda stood next to me and squeezed my hand. "Ali, may I say something."

"Oh sure."

Minda stood in front of the microphone. 'I am currently the CEO of AMN Industries here in Bacacay. I would not be here if it were not for Ali's education class. She taught me more things than I could have ever imagined. And for that, I am forever grateful."

Minda stepped away from the microphone. "Okay everyone. Do you have something to write with and paper?" Most of the students did, but there were a few who didn't.

"If you have any extra pens, pencils, and paper, could you share with the others who don't?"

After everyone was ready. "As most of you know, that in today's world, a good education is key to making yourself ready to take on what is thrown at you. Not for just today, but also for tomorrow. You have to take on challenges that has never been done before. Some of you will become doctors, scientist, run corporations, or invent a new product that will be wanted around the world. I did some of these things, but my destiny is to teach. So, lets' get started." All of the new students that was not here yesterday, you will have to take the basics when you enter college like math, sciences and english, etc.The subjects that I like are math and science. They are the key to building a foundation to anything that you are planning in your future. I will also add that learning to speak English fluently is very important. It's the international language that is spoken around the world. Okay then, let's start with science. You will take either biology or chemistry to start with." I grabbed the chalk and put up several questions on the board. After several minutes I asked who had the answer. The majority got it correct. I kept up this pace for several hours until it was decided to take a break.

Minda got up to leave. "Ali, I have to go back to work."

"I understand. Your job can be very demanding."

As Minda left, Neala stood with me as everyone left the auditorium.

I looked up at Neala. "What did you think about the first part of the class?"

"Seeing that it's hard to teach without any books for the students to follow with, you are winging it pretty good."

"Let's go and get something to eat," I said.

"Good idea. Any suggestions?" Neala asked.

"No, not really."

"Okay, let's get a pizza from Angelica's place."

On the way over to a mouthwatering pizza and a mango shake, I called Med.

"What's going on in your world?" he asked.

"Well, I've started teaching the freshman at Zamora College today. The road over to Legaspi has been severely damaged and no one knows how long before it's open. We tried to go around the long way, but the traffic is horrible. I was told by Henry, a student that wanted to start working with us, that the school buildings are completely covered in ash. We are going to have to have a good rainstorm to help wash it off."

Med didn't like hearing about his buildings in disarray. He stayed quiet for a moment. "Well, there is nothing that can be done right now. I never guessed that I would be hoping for a cyclone or a typhoon to come by and wash my buildings, but that's what looks like is going to happen to clean up the property."

"You're right about that. I never would have wished for a major storm to help with another natural disaster."

"Med, you can give Henry a call. Maybe he can work with

you on getting your buildings cleaned up."

"I'll give him a call. I could use a person to oversee my projects."

"So, Ali, how's your first day of teaching."

"Well, my class grew from one-hundred students to two-hundred in twenty-four hours."

"Say what?" Med bolstered.

"It seems word got around the province that I was going to teach the freshman class until school starts in five weeks."

"Well, if you need any help, let me know."

"That may be just what the doctor ordered," I said.

"We are on a lunch break and we'll start back up at one p.m. If you would like to stop by and see what I got myself into."

"Would love too. See you in an hour."

Neala looked at me. "What did Med have to say?"

"He will be at the school at one p.m."

After eating one of Angelica's famous pizzas and putting down one of her famous mango shakes, I was ready to take on the rest of the day. We said our goodbyes to Angie and headed back to school.

*****

Walking the hallway towards the auditorium, we found Med standing just outside the entrance door.

"Hello Ali, Neala."

"Hi Med," we replied.

With a big smile on my face, I looked up at the adults. "Let's go in and start the second half."

The three of us stood on the stage as the students began to enter the auditorium. Med seemed to have a surprised look on his face when they kept coming in and sitting down. The room was packed. "I think we picked up quite a few more students."

There were no more seats available, and more students were now standing along the walls. After everyone had returned from the lunch break, the room went quiet.

I see Mrs. Baustista and several more adults had entered the room. The look on their faces told us what they were thinking. *Where are all of these students coming from?*

The dean and her followers marched onto the stage. Standing in front of the microphone, she studied the faces of everyone in the room. "I'm curious. Where did all of the new students in here come from?" A male student stood up from his chair. "All of us from the orientation is here as well as another senior high school class that will be here next year. Due to the social media, it didn't take long for the word to spread that Ali would be teaching a class here. As soon as her name was mentioned, every student here knows who she is and what she has accomplished in a very short time."

Mrs. Bautista scratched her head. "Wow I never thought about the impact that Ali would have on the student body." She stared at everyone's face. Thinking to herself, there were at least two-hundred-and-fifty students in this room. The other faculty staff whispered to each other, "If Ali teaches here, then we'll be out of a job!" They gathered around Mrs. Baustista. After several minutes of a quiet discussion, Mrs. Baustista returned to the microphone. "Okay everyone, please quiet down. Ali will teach this class until the time that the regular classes start. Then the school will return back to normal classes."

Neala caught on to what had just happened. "I would not be allowed to teach at this college come the start of the new school year?"

"Ali, a school's administration has done it to you again. You are being ousted for being too smart." Med heard the talk that was being said around the stage between the dean and the faculty. He looked at me and left without saying a word. I saw

Alexa standing in the crowd of students. She knew that the job of teaching at this school was not going to happen and her chances of being taught by me was not going to happen now or in the distant future. I felt sorry for her. I wanted to help her, but that idea just didn't seem possible.

I stood there not knowing what to say to all of these students. I felt like I had just been told to leave the school for interacting with students all over again. Neala watched me as my emotions were activated. I was being hurt in my heart and there was nothing I could do about it. I stood in front center of the stage not saying a word. I turned my head so I could see the look from the dean and the faculty. Their stares could have burned holes in me. Turning back to the crowd of students. "I just wanted to let you know that I will not be able to teach at this college. My presence has disrupted the way things are done here. I still plan on teaching, but just not here."

The group of students sat in disarray. They just witnessed me being ousted from their school. Picking up my things, Neala and I left the building. We could hear in the background, as we exited, an uproar from the student body.

I sat in silence as Neala drove home. Sitting in Neala's SUV in front of my house, I didn't want to go in and sulk. Deep inside of my soul, I was mad.

"Neala, could we go and see Father Bayon. I need to speak with him."

Neala didn't say a word. For she knew that request was one of the best things I said all day.

*****

Pulling into the driveway of the church, I sauntered at a slow pace with my head lowered. Entering the building, I noticed that it seemed emptied. I sat near the entrance door and bowed my head. "Lord, I feel rejected by my peers because of the wonderful gift you gave me. I feel like that I'm not wanted at any school because of what I can teach. I have no one else who I can turn to." I didn't hear Father Bayon come up and stand next to where I was seated.

In a low voice, "Hello Ali. May I sit next to you?"

I looked up slowly. In a soft mellow voice, "Hello Father." A tear formed in my eyes. "Father, I keep failing. I was told that I could not teach at Zamora College. That I'm not wanted."

Father Bayon picked up my hand. "No, my child. You have not failed. The path you seek is not where you think it is. You must travel a different way in order to find what you desire."

The three of us sat in silence for several minutes.

"Ali, do you have any plans for this afternoon?"

"No Father, I have no place to go. Our school in Legaspi cannot open right now."

"Well then. Would you like to go with me to the orphanage? I have to make my rounds and I stop there every week to checkup on the children."

My mind was in high gear, but my body wouldn't move as I stared into emptiness. "I would like that Father."

Neala looked at us. "I'll drive."

*****

Father Bayon introduced us to the headmaster of the Albay Children's Home, a Ms. Flores. "This is Ali Cruz and her friend Neala."

"How do you do?" Ms. Flores asked.

"I'm fine," I said.

I could see Father Bayon with his hands together. "Ali, I'm going to make my rounds to see the children. Would you like to join me?"

"Yes Father, I would like that," I said.

The four of us headed out back of the main building to where the kids were playing. As soon as they saw the Father, everyone came around him putting his right hand to their forehead and then gave him a hug. He knelt down in front of the smaller children holding their hands and smiling at them. He then gave them each a hug. At first, I didn't notice but there was a girl sitting at a table who didn't get up to see the Father.

I locked eyes with her. We stared at each other for several seconds. I couldn't stop watching her. Ms. Flores saw what I was staring at.

"Her name is Chesah Torres. She can't walk and that is why she's not here playing with the rest of the children."

"May I go and speak to her?"

Ms. Flores looked down at me. "She would like that."

I made my way over to the table where Chesah was sitting.

"May I sit with you?" I asked.

"If you want," she said.

I could see that she was in a wheelchair. Her legs were bent at an awkward angle from the rest of her torso. "How old are you?"

She stayed quiet for several moments. I think she was trying to figure me out.

"I'm thirteen. Or I will be in four-months and three-days."

"My name is Ali."

"I know who you are. I've seen you on the news channels."

I was about to say something when my phone rang. It was from the weather service.

"Excuse me for a moment while I answer this call."

"Ali, this is Mr. Perez from the PAGASA. I just wanted to inform you that your predictions were correct about the typhoon Basil. I would like to speak with you again sometime in the future."

"Okay. Right now, I'm busy but we can talk again."

Chesah studied my facial expressions.

"Anything important?" she asked.

"I went to the PAGASA offices a couple of days ago in Queson City. I made a prediction about a typhoon that is about to hit the coastline of the Northern Salmar. My prediction was correct and now they want to talk to me again."

"Sounds like they didn't like that a young person, such as yourself, take the so-called experts down a notch or two."

"I think you may be right."

Chesah rolled her chair around the table to where I was sitting. "Want to come to my room?"

"I would like that. But first, I need to let Neala know."

"Neala, I'm going with Chesah to her room for a few minutes."

Neala stopped talking and stood next to me.

Chesah looked at me. "Who's she?"

"Neala is my dear friend and bodyguard."

"A bodyguard. What for?"

"Well, President Datu has assigned her to me."

"You know the president?"

"I do," I said smiling.

Chesah began to roll her chair away from the playground with Neala and me following her. We entered a lengthy dorm building making our way to the last door on the left. Chesah opened the door and wheeled herself inside. Standing inside of her room, I could see on her walls where there were pictures of singers, musical groups, and celebrities. But centered on her wall across from her bed was her largest image. It was Albert Einstein.

I became intrigued. "Do you like to study Albert Einstein?"

Chesah didn't say a thing. She moved over to a cabinet and opened the doors. Inside it was full of books on sciences, mathematics, and the universe.

I was liking this girl even more.

"I like to read and study everything that I can get my hands on. But here, there is not much we can get. Our internet service is limited, and I have to use the computer in the main office when it works."

"How many people stay here at this home?" I asked.

"Right now, there are thirty-two. A few of the younger kids may be adopted by a family, but kids like me will never have a real family or a place to call home."

I had a sad feeling when I heard her speak. I told myself, "we sure take a lot of things in life for granted."

"Do you go to school?"

Chesah didn't answer me at first. "I did when I was five, but my health kept me from attending. After I lost my parents that same year, no other family member would take me in because I'm in a wheelchair. I'm too much trouble to deal with they said. So here I am."

"I too lost my real parents when I was a baby. I'm adopted and so is my best friend and half-sister Minda. She now lives with me and my adopted parents."

Chesah smiled. "I read about her on the internet. Isn't she now the CEO of a large company here in Bacacay?"

"She is. I put her there. I started that company four years ago. But my dream is to teach. So, I walked away from the large company and now I'm looking for a place that I can fit in. Our Lord gave me the gift of knowledge and I want to use it to teach others."

"How did you learn to read?" I asked.

"I had some help from Ms. Flores, but most of what I learned, I taught myself."

"You sound like me," I said.

"Can you teach us here? But first you would have to ask the people in charge."

"I know that's right," I said.

We left Chesah's room and headed back outside to where Father Bayon and Ms. Flores were.

"Ali, what do you think?" Father Bayon asked.

Everyone that was in ear shot focused their eyes on me. I stood there for several seconds with a gazed look on my face. A thought came to mind. I think Father Bayon must have had good intentions when he asked me to come along to the orphanage. He knew that I would find students here to teach. "Well, if Ms. Flores and the other administrators here and the people who run this home would like for me to teach here, then I would like to work with the students. That is, if they would want me?"

I needed to hear from everyone who lives here. Another rejection would crush me.

Every student stood up and shouted. "Teach us. Teach us." Even Chesah tried to stand. That gave me the feeling that I so desired, to be wanted.

"If the administrators call me and tell me that it's okay, then I'll be here."

# ~Chapter Fifteen~

Staying at home and waiting for my phone to ring cannot make for a productive day. Neala watched me as I wondered about looking for something to occupy my mind. She knew that I had a billion electrical impulses in my brain firing at once. I turned to face her, "I have been holding in my emotions for too long. I need to let it out or I'm going to regret what I might say to someone."

"Neala, can you take me over to see Father Bayon?"

"Sure, let's go."

Standing in the doorway of Saint Rose of Lima Parish Church, I had to wait several seconds for my eyes to adjust to the darkened room. Squinting my eyes, I watched Father Bayon go about his business of cleaning the pews and putting reading materials back into their places.

"Good morning, Father," I said as I strolled up to where he was working.

"Good morning, Ali. How are you today?"

"I'm fine."

Neala walked in and sat down on a rear pew.

"Hello Neala," Father Bayon spoke with a bold voice.

"Good morning, Father."

"Father, I need to speak to a person like yourself."

"I'm always here for you."

"Father, it seems that every time I try to start to teach others, I'm being stopped by just about everybody. I've been told that I cannot teach here or all the other teachers will quit. That's why I had to leave Switzerland. Now, I have been told at Zamora College the same thing." My emotions kicked in and tears ran down my face. "I feel like I'm not wanted anywhere in this world. It's like, I'm an outcast because of my brain." I began to sob uncontrollably.

Father Bayon knew that I needed to vent out what was building up inside of me. He also knew that if I didn't let it out, it would take control of me and I might do something horrible, and I would regret it for the rest of my life. He stayed silent until I finally said my peace.

"Ali, people are afraid of you. They don't intentionally go about trying to hurt you. But you have a great advantage over them and they don't like it. That's why they asked you to leave their school. I knew that something like this was going to happen to you. That's why I asked you to go with me to the orphanage. I thought it might be the right place for you to follow your dream. Lord knows the kids there would leave one day with an education that no school could ever match."

Looking up at his face, I inquired, "Have you heard anything from the directors of the orphanage?"

Father Bayon removed his glasses and cleaned them with his shirt. "Not yet, but I would almost bet they will be calling soon. When a rare opportunity such as this comes along, you don't just let it pass you by. That would be foolish on their part."

I got up to leave. "Thank you, Father, for listening to me vent."

"Ali, I'm always here for you."

"Thanks again, Father."

I was just about ready to open the car door when my phone rang. It was Ms. Flores. "Ali, we have been given permission for you to come and teach here."

My whole being was full of joy. Tears dripped down my

face. Turning towards the church, I saw Father Bayon smiling. He already knew.

I looked at Neala. She also knew that I had found my place in this world.

"Neala, may we go..." I didn't have to finish what I was thinking. She just smiled.

"Get in."

*****

We had just rolled up to the front of the Albay Children's Home when we were greeted by the full body of students and adults.

Chesah rolled her chair up to where I was standing. She reached slowly and took my hand. "Thanks for coming back. I prayed that you might return to teach us." Suddenly, I was surrounded by children ranging from ages of three to seventeen. I heard the most precious little girl's voice and I looked down to see a child of no more than three-years-old looking up at me. "Thank you, Ali, for helping us." I had tears beginning to flow down my face. She saw my facial reaction. She too began to cry. "Did I make you sad?" she asked.

"Oh no!" I replied, kneeling down in front of her to wipe her tears away. "You've made me very happy."

I looked up at the heavens. I knew with all of my soul that I just found my place in this world where I am truly wanted.

Neala made her way to where I was standing. Putting her arm around my shoulder, I looked up at her face. She had red eyes as well. She knew that this was the place where I was supposed to be.

Ms. Flores waved her hand. "Okay, let's go inside and show Ali our home." The little girl that I had talked to and a young boy of about four-years-old took my hands. They walked me into a large room that had a blackboard on one wall and all of the desks were lined up against several walls.

I felt a tug on my right hand. The little girl looked up at me. "I sit over there in that chair," pointing with her little finger.

"That's wonderful." I said. "Do you like to go to school?" She smiled, "I do."

"By the way, what is your name?" I asked.

"My name is Dalisay."

The little boy tugged on my other hand. "My name is Joselito. And I sit over there." "That's great," I said while smiling at both of them.

I was listening to everyone trying to talk at the same time when my phone rang. It was Med.

"Ali, where are you? I went by your home, but nobody is there."

"I'm at the Albay Children's Home. Father Bayon brought me here yesterday. I have been asked to teach the children." Med stayed silent.

"Ali, I'll be there in a few minutes."

"Okay," I said as I hung up.

Neala looked at me. "What's up?"

"Med is coming by in a few minutes."

It took less than fifteen minutes when we heard a buzzer ring. Ms. Flores opened the door to Med.

"May I help you?" Ms. Flores asked.

"I'm here to see Ali."

"Ali, you have a visitor."

Making my way over to where they were standing, I looked into the faces of both adults.

"Ms. Flores, this is Dr. Med Montoya. He was the chief surgeon at the hospital here."

"Nice to meet you, Ms. Flores." Med smiled and shook her hand. Then Med turned to face me. "Ali, what's up?"

"Well Med, I have been asked to teach here at the children's home. I went to visit Father Bayon yesterday and he brought me here."

"I see. So, what are you going to do with the buildings that we were going to use to start a school?"

"I have thought about it a lot. With the way things have turned out for us, starting our school is not a good business decision. I think that it's best that we put that on hold for now. We cannot travel to the school buildings without going the long way around the Mayon. Neala and I tried to make it. After almost six hours of sitting in traffic and not going just a few kilometers and the school buildings cannot be inhabited without having to breathe the ash that has accumulated on them, that alone would be an extreme health hazard. I have made a decision that our school is not ready to be occupied. It seems we have come up against every roadblock that could be thrown at us."

Med seemed a little distraught. He had a lot of money invested in the Seafare Hotel buildings. He knew what I was saying about the health hazards that comes from having to breathe this ash. Being a businessman, he also knew that sometimes things just don't work out the way you had planned for. He may one day be able to use the buildings or sell them.

"Med, I'm so sorry that the Seafare Hotel did not pan out for you."

"Well, Ali, things sometimes happen in the real estate market. It's part of doing business. Let's just put that business aside for now. Is there anything that I can do to help you?"

"Well for starters, do you still have the computers that you purchased?"

"I do."

"May we use them here? They only have one and it's an old model that's very slow."

"Okay, what else?"

"Can you help me teach the older students? There are five, I think."

Ms. Flores jumped into the conversation, "We do have five from ages fifteen to seventeen."

Med's face seemed to light up a bit. "May I speak to these students?"

"Oh sure," Ms. Flores replied. She then asked an assistant to go and get them from their rooms.

Several minutes later, three girls and two boys appeared. Med stood waiting for them to arrive. As soon as they entered the room, Med smiled. "Good day."

They all replied. "Good day to you, sir."

"My name is Dr. Med Montoya. I was recently the head of surgery at Memorial Hospital here in Bacacay. I just retired from there about two months ago. Now, I am helping Ali with teaching and she has asked me to work with you five."

A sixteen-year-old boy named Alfred spoke up. "I would like to study medicine and become a doctor. The other four focused on Alfred. Then the three girls replied. "We would like to be nurses." Med liked what he was hearing. "I can help you four achieve your dreams." The oldest boy who was seventeen didn't say a thing. He seemed bored with the conversation the others were having.

Med locked eyes with him. "What about you?" He looked away. "I just want to get out of here and go away."

Med concentrated on him for several minutes. "What is your name?"

"It's Juan. Juan Gonzales."

"Okay Juan. What do you like to do?"

"Nothing," he replied.

"Oh, come now Juan. There is something in this world that brings you satisfaction when you achieve it."

Juan stayed quiet. Everyone in the room locked their eyes

on him. He scanned the faces of his fellow roommates. Juan felt embarrassed talking in front of everyone. Ms. Flores knew that Juan didn't say much to anybody. "He always kept to himself."

Med stayed quiet for several seconds. "Juan, I'm not picking on you. As with all people, there is something that we dream of doing with our lives. That's what makes us human."

I watched Juan's body movements. He began to relax with us a little. "I like to sing and dance," he said. Everyone's eyes locked in.

"Can you sing something for us?" Med asked.

Juan didn't say a thing. He stayed quiet for several more seconds. He thought about his life and how it was going nowhere. He looked straight at me. With a determined look on his face, he let out what has been bothering him too long. "Now is the time." I knew that he was beginning to unravel his tight web that he had wrapped himself with. The room went quiet. Juan closed his eyes and began to sing "Hallelujah." with a soft gentle voice. Then it hit him as he opened himself up and let out the voice that had been hidden for so long. Everyone was taken back as we listened to this young man's beautiful voice. The whole room was mesmerized at the sound coming from within him.

"Oh my," I said. "Where have you been hiding that beautiful voice? The world needs to hear you." Juan seemed really embarrassed now.

"Well, I don't like to sing in front of people."

Med moved in front of Juan. Taking his hands, Med looked into his eyes. "Juan, after singing that beautiful song, I have to believe that you're a Christian and our Lord has brought you to us."

Juan looked down at the floor. Then he returned his gaze into Med's eyes. "No more." he kept saying. "No more." With pride and jubilation in his voice "I am. I'm a Christian."

"Then my friend, you are about to discover the world that

you have only dreamed about."

I looked at the other children. One by one I asked each person what he or she would like to be or do when they grow up. One special little girl who had a handicapped right hand, spoke up. "I would like to play the piano. But my handicap won't let me." I saw a tear form in her eye as she looked at her right arm.

"You may have a handicap, but never let that stop you from believing in yourself and what you can do. I truly believe that anything is possible, if you want it bad enough and try as hard as you can to make it happen."

A ten-year-old boy replied. "We don't have a piano here."

Ms. Flores listened to what the children were saying. "We can't afford a piano."

"If I can get one, will you let the children play on it?" I asked.

Ms. Flores didn't know what to say. "But of course. If we had one, that would be a wonderful thing for them to learn about music."

Med overheard the conversation that I was having with Ms. Flores. He walked into another room and made a few phone calls.

As soon as he returned, he stood next to me and Ms. Flores. "Where would you put a piano? In this room or is there another place?"

"We have another room about half of this size that we use to store things."

"May we see it?" I asked.

Ms. Flores took us to the other room. It was full of all kinds of stuff.

Med looked at everything. "Do you use any of these things?"

Ms. Flores replied. "No, not really. Just the Christmas decorations."

"If we can get the room cleaned, may we put a piano in here?"

Ms. Flores didn't know what to say at first. "You would do that for us?"

Med smiled. "I would. Instead of a storage room, it would become your music room."

Ms. Flores liked the sound of that. "I think that music would bring some happiness to these children's lives."

"Med, do you play the piano?" I asked.

"As a matter of fact, I do. I have been playing since I was five."

"Then, would you teach anyone who wants to learn?"

"I would like that very much," he said with a very large smile on his face.

"Okay then. Ms.Flores would you go and takeout anything in your new music room that you would get rid of."

"I sure will. I've been wanting to do just that for many years." She stopped for a moment and scratched her head. "Why am I doing this if we don't have a piano?"

Med smiled at her. "I have already bought one and it should be here this afternoon."

"Oh my. No one has ever done something this nice for the children before. Thank you for being so kind and generous."

"You're welcome, Ms. Flores. Would you like to tell everyone?"

"I would. They need to know about everything that goes on here. I made them a promise that I would never lie or hide the truth about anything that may have an influence on their lives."

"I like the sound of that," I said.

Chesah rolled her chair towards me. "Can I help you with anything?"

I thought for a moment. "You can be my assistant and help me teach the class about science and math."

Chesah's face started to glow. I could see her cheeks turning a darker shade of red.

"I would like that a lot. When do we start?"

"How about now?" I said.

With every person at this school gathered in the big room, I stood in front of the group. "What books do you have here right now?"

Several of the administrators went to gather up what was available. After a five-minute wait, they returned with just a few books. Looking at the small stack, there were a couple of preschool books, a few elementary, and a couple for high school. After making notes on the titles, I pulled out my phone and went online to a school bookstore. After about a ten-minute ordeal, I bought enough books and several more just in case a new child may come into this home.

"Okay everyone, I just purchased enough books for us to work with and a few more just in case of any new students. I also added a few college-level books that Chesah and few of you may find interesting. I have them being shipped for overnight delivery."

Ms. Flores and the two other administrators didn't know what to say. They never had a budget to buy books or anything else like this. And now, a young girl and a man who are strangers have done just that.

Ms. Flores and two of her helpers left to go and clean out the new music room.

Returning my attention to the children, they began to volley questions at me. "Are you famous? Are you rich? How old are you? Who sent you here and so on?"

"That's a lot of questions to ask at once. But, I will do my best to answer each of them. Am I famous? Depends on who you ask. I am one of the few people from around the world who is known for having a very high IQ. Am I rich? To some, they would say so, but to others, the answer would be no, and to who sent me here? And as far as my age, well I'm nine-years-old. It was Father Bayon who brought me here to see you. But I truly believe that our Lord and Savior Jesus Christ is the one who sent me here. He gave me a special gift when I was four-years-old. It was the gift of knowledge. I have been putting that gift to work by helping people here and in our country. Now I want to teach students like yourselves. Maybe one day, you may do the same and help others who are in need."

"Okay everyone, let's divide up into groups. All preschool children will gather here where I am standing right now." Then I pointed at another location within the room. "All elementary students will meet there." Pointing yet to another location, "all high school students will meet over there. This way I can see what we need to work on. Preschoolers need the basics of reading and writing skills. The elementary students will need to work on science, math, english and maybe music, if they are so inclined. The high school students will need to work on the same, but in more depth, especially in math and science. If any of you want to study music and learn how to sing, maybe Juan would like to help in that department."

Juan smiled. "I can do that."

"Since I don't know what schooling any of you may or may not have taken or are going to school now for the first time, Med and I will ask each of you questions so we can get a feel of where you're at in your education."

Writing down notes on each student, we came to the conclusion that schooling is not something that these students are getting much of. "Okay everyone. Since we only have a few books to work with, the preschoolers can use the books that are here for now. There should be enough to go around. I'll take the elementary students and that leaves the high school students with Med. Chesah, I need to work with you for a moment. Can you bring some paper and something to write with?"

Chesah rolled herself to where I was seated. "May I use

your paper for a moment?" She reached out and handed it to me.

"How far along are you in math and science? Can you work on calculus, algebra, trigonometry, and geometry? And how far are you in the sciences."

"I have studied all of the different types of math along with biology, physics, and astronomy."

"I'm going to write down some math problems and science questions. I just need to know what area's we need to work in. Please don't get upset with me since we have never worked together. This will help me understand your strong and weak points."

I began to write down several pages of math problems and science questions.

I handed the notepad back to her. She glanced down at the paper. Wheeling her chair to a table, she put her mind to work on the problems I gave her.

I turned my attention to the preschoolers. Handing them some paper and a pencil, I had them working on the alphabet and their numbers. Then I gathered up the elementary students. I wrote some math problems and science questions down for them to work on.

I had just turned in my chair when Chesah rolled herself to my chair. "I finished everything you asked me to do."

"May I," pointing at her notepad.

She handed me her paper. I studied each of her answers. "Very good. Some of these math problems are taught in college. Would you like to work in college-level books?"

Chesah smiled. "I would. That would be a challenge for me."

"You sound like me. I have always challenged myself to do something that I have never seen or done before. That is the only way you will ever exceed in life. You must push yourself to the next level. I'm going to give you a problem that NASA had to solve on the ISS last year. I like to use this as an example because these are real problems that have to be solved in order to ward off any danger to the ISS. This particular problem took their scientist several hours to solve. See if you can?"

After writing the problem down, I returned her notepad. She looked at what I had just written. Rolling back to the table, I saw her turn her head and smile. She studied the problem that I gave her. Watching her tackle the situation that I put in front of her, she wanted to prove to me that she was for real. She was not afraid to take on something she'd never seen before. Returning my attention to the preschoolers, I asked each person to show me what they put down on their paper. Moving next to each child, I had them work on writing their numbers and letters. I turned myself towards the elementary students.

"Let me see what you have written?" After viewing each person's paper, I gave them some more equations to work on, when suddenly, I felt a tap on my arm. Chesah had finished the problem-solving equation I gave her. Taking her notepad, I looked at her answer. She had solved the problem in less than ten minutes.

"That's fantastic. You're correct. How did you come up with your answer?"

Chesah stared at her paper as she explained, "I had to use geometry, calculus, and astrophysics to calculate my answer."

"Very good," I said. "I can see a bright future for you in the aerospace industry. They are looking for people with your intelligence as we progress into the twenty-first century."

"Do you think they would take someone like me since I cannot walk?"

"That has nothing to do with the knowledge you carry in your mind. Have you ever heard of Steven Hawking?"

"I have," she said. "That never stopped him from doing what he loved. He was paralyzed from the neck down and still was able to teach classes at a university."

"Just because you are confined to a chair, don't ever let that stop you from following your dreams. Nobody can ever take that away from you."

Chesah looked at me and smiled. "Thanks, Ali, for this confidence talk."

"You are welcome. I too sometimes have to talk to someone. Our feelings and emotions are what makes us human."

I continued working with the students until late in the afternoon. Looking at Neala, she just smiled. It gave her pleasure watching me with the kids. I didn't realize that we had skipped lunch today. My stomach began to make its growling noises.

"Okay everyone. It's nearly five o'clock. The piano was supposed to be delivered today but I guess we will just have to wait until tomorrow. Med, Neala and I will be back here at seven-thirty tomorrow morning. Then we will continue where we left off."

The three of us gathered our things and we said our goodbyes to everyone.

Making our way at a slow pace towards our parked cars, Med looked at me. "I never would have thought about working at an orphanage, but after seeing the children, I'm beginning to like the idea. A good education would allow them to follow their dreams."

I touched Med's hand. "Thanks for helping me with this. I still think about the students at Zamora College, but I don't want to create any problems for anybody there. I don't want to be where I'm not wanted. Maybe someday, I can help them, but I just don't see it in the near future."

Med squeezed my hand. "I feel like a second father to you. And I like it a lot."

Neala smiled. "I feel the same way, like a second mother as well."

I thought about this conversation. I started life with one set of parents. Then before I was one-year-old, I got a second set. Now that I'm nine, I now have a third set of parents. What's the odds in that?

# ~Chapter Sixteen~

I still have some childlike thoughts running through my head from time to time. I stood with Med and Neala in front of the Albay Children's Home front gate. I looked at both of their faces. Smiling, I made my voice a little louder than necessary. "The three musketeers are here to take on the evil villain." Both of the adults had a look of surprise at what I just said.

"Are we feeling a little childish this morning?" Neala commented.

Med just smiled. "One for all and all for one." It seems he has a little medieval influence in his blood as well.

"Med, your words take me back to Rorris Castle in Switzerland. There were paintings of knights in armor, plaques of coats of arms hanging on the walls. That castle was built in sixteen forty-eight."

Med rubbed his beard. "I would like to visit such a place and stay awhile. The history the walls contain would be fascinating lessons from our past."

"They would at that," I said. Returning my focus to what laid before us, we stood at the front door and rang the bell.

Ms. Flores answered. "Ali, you don't have to ring the bell to enter."

"I did not want to show disrespect to you or the children by just walking in."

"Thanks for being so kind. The children should be finishing

up their breakfast and shall be here shortly."

Neala moved off to the side of the room as Med and I moved the chairs around. As soon as the students arrived, we split them into their groups. I had the preschoolers working on their letters and numbers, and the elementary students working on some math and science problems.

Chesah rolled her chair up to where I was standing. "Is there anything I can do to help?"

Thinking, "give me about a couple of minutes. I need to see what students have a better grasp of the problems that I gave them, then you can help them work on their math problems."

Chesah seemed to like what I just told her, *'that someone like me was asking her for help in teaching.'* A thought came into my mind. She may become a teacher herself one day. I liked that idea a lot.

Once the fifth and sixth grade aged students finished their assignments, I knew which ones had the correct answers. There were five students who I wanted Chesah to work with.

Pulling these students off to the side, I handed Chesah a couple of books that I brought from home. The same one's that Minda had used to pass the high school exit exam. I pointed at the problems that I wanted her to work with. Watching her facial reactions as she opened the college math books, I knew that I had just challenged her. She looked at me and smiled.

I looked at her face. "Work with these students and let's see how you do."

Chesah went to the blackboard and wrote several of the problems from the book. She then explained how to work the problems that she put up on the board.

I turned back to the preschoolers to see how they were doing. After several hours, I had each of them begin to read and write the basic letters and numbers. There was one five-year-old boy named Rolado who could not only write his name, but he could read the basic sentences in their book at an alarming speed.

I think we may have a new scholar in our midst. Pulling him aside, I gave him something a little harder to work on. At first, he seemed down like I was picking on him, but I gave him a pep talk to put his mind at ease. He accepted my challenge and went to work on his writing and reading assignments.

Next up were the rest of the students. "Okay everyone, let's work on some science problems." Without any of the books that I needed, I put on the blackboard some problems and explained how to get the answers. I didn't hear the bell ring, but I saw Ms. Flores answer the door. The piano was being delivered.

"In this room." Ms. Flores directed the workers to roll in a heavy wooden box. After the movers had left, Med wanted to see what he had purchased. Studying the faces of everyone, he proceeded to sit in front of the piano. He hit a few keys slowly at first, and then the room went quiet. Med began to play some beautiful songs. The room was filled up with a wonderful sound of music. Everyone cheered after hearing the sounds that came from this musical instrument.

Med saw Juan standing in the corner. "Juan, would you like to play something?" He hesitated at first, but he knew that he must continue to concur his fears. Med rose from the bench and let Juan take over. After he hit a few keys, he began to play a few Christian songs. I heard a few sour notes being hit but he still did a great job of playing for us.

Returning to the classroom, we went back to work on solving the problems that I had assigned to each group. I heard the main doorbell ring. One of the supervisor's got up from her desk to answer the door. It was a delivery man bringing the books that I had ordered. Opening each box, I separated the books into age groups. Ms. Flores passed them out to each person. It felt good bringing a little joy to this place. The smiles on everyone's face told a wonderful story. I never heard the bell ring again over the noise the kids were making while looking at their new books. And today was the day that Father Bayon likes to come by and checkup on how the children are.

"Hello, Father," I said putting the back side of his right hand to my forehead.

"Hello, Ali. How's everything going so far?"

"It's going great. We just received the books that I had ordered and the piano that Med bought was delivered this morning as well."

"Books and a piano. My, my. That was genuinely nice of you and Med."

"Med believes that music is great for the soul and it will help the children. He was right."

"May I show you what we have been working on?"

"Oh, please do."

I took Father Bayon to the new music room. "This use to be a storage closet, now the students have a music room. And back in the classroom, Med and I have separated the students into different groups. He's working with the older students on sciences and the different medical fields and I'm working with the rest. I have divided them up into different groups. Preschoolers, elementary, and high school. There are a few high school kids that seem to be upper achievers. I have an extraordinary student who is helping me with them as well. Her name is Chesah."

"I know her. Isn't she the young lady in the wheelchair?"

"She is and she's very intelligent. She wants to help me work with the students, so I gave her a job of helping the upper achievers."

"How is that working out?"

"See for yourself. We watched Chesah explain the problem, "What does it take to solve the problem and where might such a problem exist in the world?"

Raising my voice. "Okay everyone. Father Bayon has

stopped by to see how everyone is doing." Each student came up to him and put his right hand to their forehead. Afterwards, they returned to their seats. Chesah rolled her chair next to him. Father Bayon picked up Chesah right hand and held it for several seconds. I heard him speak softly to her.

It didn't take Father Bayon very long to pick up on Rolado. He was mumbling to himself at an extremely fast speed. Stopping in front of his desk, Father Bayon knelt down so he could face Rolado at eye level. "I heard you speaking to yourself. Can you read that fast?"

Rolado shrugged his shoulders. "I guess so," he said.

"Can you read to me the part that you just read?" He looked down at his book and then looked back to the Father. He began to read. Afterwards, Father Bayon looked up at me then back at Rolado. "How old are you?"

"I'm five-years-old."

Father Bayon stood up and placed his hand on Rolando's head. "Ali, you need to work with him. We may just have another you here in our mist."

Ms. Flores looked at Rolado. "Do you understand what you just read?"

"Yes." He began to explain in detail everything that he read to Father Bayon.

Father Bayon picked up a high school history book. "Rolado, can you read me the first chapter? I will follow along with you in this book."

Rolado began to read about how Spain had power in the Philippines for over three-hundred years. After a few minutes, Rolado shut his book. He began to explain in detail what he had just read.

Father Bayon found a chair and sat down. Removing his glasses, he pulled out a handkerchief so he could clean the lenses.

"Ali, I have been coming to this children's home for many

years and I never knew how intelligent these students are. I can just imagine what they will be capable of after been taught by you and Med."

Father Bayon went back to talking to the children. I looked around the room for Neala, but I could not find her anywhere in site.

Opening the breakroom door, I found her with a cup of coffee in her hands. "Hey," I said searching for another coffee cup.

She smiled at me as she turned on a television.

"What's up?" I asked.

"Just wanting to check up on the weather report."

I knew what she was thinking and that she was right. It's always good to check everyday for any developments in the Pacific. Storms can flare up at any time. After the national and local news had aired, a weather bulletin came onto the screen.

*"We have a weather alert,"* the newscaster said.

*"The PAGASA has just released a satellite view of some disturbing weather just off the coast of Dinagat. We will be able to tell you more as soon as we get word from the weather service. Please stay tuned on any future developments."*

Neala reached up to turn off the television when my phone rang. It was Mr. Perez from the weather service.

"Ali, have you heard about our latest development?"

"I just saw the weather report on the television."

"If I send you the information that we have received so far, can you look at it and give me your best estimate about any future developments?"

"I sure will. Here is my email address. Send it to me and I'll get back with you."

Mr. Perez replied. "Okay, thanks."

After several minutes, Neala and I returned to the group.

"Okay everyone. I have just been sent some information

about a storm that is starting to develop off the coast of Dinagat."

"Where's that?" a ten-year-old girl asked.

Finding a large map of the Philippines in a storage closet, I discussed each section of our country. Starting with Luzon, Visayas, and then Mindanao. I pointed to the place I was told about. "I have been asked by the National Weather Service named PAGASA to give them my prediction about this new disturbance. It will not have a name until its development is better defined."

Opening up my laptop, I pulled up the information that was emailed to me. A large group of curious students surrounded me. I looked over my right shoulder to see students moving out of the way so Chesah could roll her chair next to me. "Take a look at the information that was just sent to me and tell me what you think." She studied the maps, wind direction, temperature of the ocean water, time of year and anything else that would be a determining factor. She looked up at me. In a calm positive note, "I know what this disturbance is going to do." She moved back out of the way so the others could see my computer screen and work on the problem. As each student studied the information, they moved out of the way so the others could review my computer screen. After the last student studied the problem, I went to the blackboard.

"Okay everyone. This is a real-life problem that needs to be solved as quickly as possible. People can be killed by this storm if the information is not correct. They will not have time to move out of the way of the approaching storm. Will each person who studied the notes that was sent to me, tell us your prediction about this disturbed weather?" As each one told their prediction, I made notes onto the blackboard.

Then I turned to Chesah. "You said that you know what this storm will do. Care to elaborate on your prediction?"

"This storm will travel into Leyte Gulf, build into a cyclone, move north by northwest and skirt along the Albay Province. We will get heavy rains but not a lot of winds from it."

"Can you tell us how you came up with your prediction?" I asked.

"Well, after looking at the notes you have on your laptop, I read the water temperature, the wind direction, the barometric pressure of the upper and lower atmosphere, and time of year."

"Okay class. What Chesah has predicted is almost correct. The time of year has a lot to determine where the earth's location is to the sun and its orbit around it. Different times of the year, we have stronger winds such as in early March through April. We have the monsoon season as well. That's when we have the heaviest rains almost everyday. What Chesah didn't take into consideration is the wind speed that is coming off the east coast of Indonesia. At its current speed, the upper winds will reach us by midnight tonight and that will cause the low-pressure area above Eastern Salmar to pull this storm along its coastline and it will turn and head towards Sorsogon. Legaspi City will take a direct hit and so will we. We have two days to get prepared for it."

Chesah didn't say a word. I had just corrected her and that hit a nerve. I walked over to her and put my hand on hers. "Your prediction was particularly good. I saw the mistake that you overlooked is all." She didn't say a thing.

Then she looked up at me. "Do you think that I will ever be as smart as you?"

"I truly believe that you have a remarkably high IQ. And there will be schools or businesses that will be wanting your services to help them prosper."

"Do you think somebody, or some place will want me? You know since I'm in this wheelchair."

"Your chair is not what they want. It's your knowledge and what you can bring to the table is what's important. You can teach others, or make a company grow. That's what they want from you. Someday, you will have your own place that you purchased from all of the hard work you put in. You may become married to a wonderful person as well."

She smiled. "Let's not get too mussy with all of this married stuff." She let out a small giggle.

I smiled back. "I have only known you for a couple of days and I see a very intelligent person. I'm going to let you use the college books that I have. Study them after school when you have the time. These are the same books that I let Minda use, and she now has her B.A. from the University of the Philippines, and she is now CEO of the company I started. Not bad considering that she received her bachelors degree at the age of nine." Crossing my arms. "You remind me a lot of her. A person who will not take no for an answer. To coin a phrase from the Apollo missions, *"Failure Is Not an Option."*

I didn't notice Ms. Flores was standing near me. She had her head turned so she could hear me give Chesah a pep talk. The Apollo mission phrase must have caught her attention because I saw her making notes to have a banner about it hanging above the door.

# ~Chapter Seventeen~

Picking up my phone, I made a call to Mr. Peez. "Ali, I'm glad you called back. What are your predictions for this weather disturbance?"

"Has it been named yet?" I asked.

"It just has. It will be called Claudio."

"I kept quiet for several seconds. I think that this storm will cross Sorsogon and hit Legaspi City. Then it will track northwest hitting us here in Bacacay. I would say that we have approximately twenty-four hours before hitting Sorsogon. Oh, by the way, I'm at the Albay Children's Home here in Bacacay and there is a very intelligent girl here named Chesah. I showed her your notes, and she came up with most of this prediction."

"Just how old is this girl?"

"She's twelve," I said.

"You don't say? I would like to meet this person one day. We are always looking for very bright people for our future."

"I will pass it along to her."

"Let me know what your team comes up with or my prediction is correct. I would like to tell Chesah that she had a part in saving people's lives."

"I will call you as soon as we can put out the information."

I called Mayor Manalo.

"Ali, it's good to hear from you. How've you been?"

"I'm fine sir. I've started teaching here at the Albay

Children's Home."

"I heard from Father Bayon. Good for you! They will become very prosperous people in their future with the education they'll receive."

"Sir, why I am calling is that I have been talking to Mr. Perez with the PAGASA Office in Queson City about a storm that has just been named Claudio. I've predicted that it will hit Sorsogon and then us. Mr. Perez is checking with his people to see if my prediction is correct or if it will hit somewhere else. The information has not gone out yet but will shortly. I think that we only have less than twenty-four hours before landfall."

"That doesn't give us much time to prepare. I'll check with the emergency manage+ment team for any updates. Thanks, Ali, for the heads up. I will call you when I hear any news."

After I hung up, I called a meeting with the whole school. "As some of you know, a cyclone named Claudio has formed in the Leyte Gulf. Chesah and I have made a prediction that I gave to the PAGASA weather group. They are checking to see we are correct or their meteorologist." I caught the smile on Chesah's face. "They will let me know if we are in immediate threat from this storm."

"Ms. Flores, what are the schools plans when dealing with these storms?"

"We head to the shelters when we are told to leave."

"That sounds like a great plan. Chesah and I will let you know what is happening at any time day or night."

"Thank you, Ali, for helping us."

"You're welcome. Do any of the students here have a cell phone?"

"No. We don't allow any student to have one here. It's best because every child would want one and we just cannot afford to have them."

"I understand. By any chance, do you have a cell phone?"

"I do. I only use it for emergencies."

'May I have your phone number? I may need to call you in the middle of the night if I hear any information about a storm or anything else."

"Oh sure."

I put her phone number into my cell and gave her mine, Neala's and Med's.

"Ali. I been meaning to ask you about Neala. Just who is she and why does she follow you everywhere?"

"Neala is my bodyguard. She was assigned to me by President Datu. Because of my gift of knowledge, I have had several people wanting to kidnap me for their illicit ideas. She has become an awfully close friend and a second mother to me. She now has her own security company and is still in close contact with the president and the secret service."

"I see. That makes you an important person to the government."

"I never thought of it that way, but I guess it does."

"Please don't go and tell everyone. I have had enough troubles because of what I know."

"I won't say a word." Ms. Flores said.

"Thanks. Let's get back to teaching." I pulled my group together and Med gathered up his. Starting with the preschoolers, I had each of them read aloud from their book. Sitting on the floor with these students, Dalisay looked up at my face.

"Ali, would you adopt me?"

Those words triggered some very deep emotions within my soul. I felt a tear run down my face. I mumbled with soft words. "I can't, I'm only nine-years-old." I wanted to tell her that I too was adopted, but to a three-year-old, she wouldn't understand. I sat next to her small body while looking into her eyes, and I could see a tear on her beautiful face as well. I picked up her tiny hands and held them. "I will ask around to see if someone would step up and take you into their home. Let's get back to working on our schoolwork, okay?"

Returning my attention to the elementary students, I asked to borrow a book from a student closest to me. Scanning each page at my normal reading speed, I finished his book in just a couple of minutes. I didn't notice the look on everybody's face, but I think I saw a few mouths open. One high school girl pointed at the book in my hands. "Did you just finish that book?"

I looked down at it. "Why yes," I said.

'How did you do that?" she asked.

Setting the book down on the desk that was in front of me, I looked up at the faces of the students. "I was given the gift of knowledge by our Lord. I can read at an extraordinary rate of speed. I have been able to do that since I was four-years -old."

"Can you teach us to read at that speed?"

I paused for a moment. "Reading at a high speed is not what is important. The main thing is understanding what you have just read and putting that knowledge to use. Med cannot read at the speed that I can, but he can bring out the knowledge that you will need in the medical field or any other field that you may choose to go into."

An idea hit me. "Med, lets join the upper elementary students with the high school students and cover all the subjects that they will need to pass the exit exams. The younger elementary students and the preschoolers will continue as they are now."

I was about to start the class when I heard my cell phone ring in my briefcase. It was Mr. Perez.

"Ali, after going over your notes on typhoon Claudio, our computer models predict the same as you do. What makes it so strange is that you had the information two hours before any computer could. The information is going out as we speak. You need to plan for an evacuation now. The eye will pass directly over you in about fourteen hours. Stay safe. We need to talk again after the storm has passed."

"Okay. Thanks for the heads up," I said.

I summoned everyone to the classroom. "Is this everyone?" Ms. Flores seemed a little perturbed that I asked such a question.

I stayed quiet for several seconds. "I just got off of the phone with the PAGASA Weather Service and the cyclone named Claudio is now a typhoon and we're going to take a direct hit. We have approximately fourteen hours. That's why I asked to have everyone present. This information is too important." The look on Ms. Flores face said it best. She knew that I was looking out for everyone's well-being. I called Minda, Father Bayon and Mayor Manalo.

Chesah rolled her chair up to where I was standing. I looked at her face. "Our prediction was right." She smiled. "We may have saved a person's life."

I smiled back at her. "If we saved anybody's life, then it was worth any effort that we put into it. I was told that we beat the computers by two hours. Mr. Perez, Director of Operations there wants to talk to us after the storm is over."

Chesah began to run her fingers through her hair. "I wonder what that is all about."

"He may invite us to visit his office to discuss how we knew more than his computers."

"Do you mean we get to fly?"

"Yes. I visited him last month, and that's why he called me when another storm had developed. Lead time is extremely important when you need to get out of the way of these things."

Ms. Flores waved her arms. "Okay, listen up. Go to your room and grab your backpacks. Put your schoolbooks into it and a change of clothes. Pick up a bottle of water and a snack as we leave the building. Let's not wait until this storm is upon us before we get prepared to leave. I will not take any chance that someone will be left behind." Watching Ms. Flores direct the kids, and giving them sound advice, I knew that she loved each and every one as if they were her own. You could not ask for a better mother than she. I'm so proud to know her.

Since it was getting close to lunch time, a meal was prepared for the students.

"Ali, would you, Med, and Neala like to join us for lunch? It may be the only meal we get today." We thanked her for inviting us to join them.

"Before we eat, may I say a blessing?"

Ms. Flores seemed a little surprised that I offered to say a blessing. "Oh, please do. We would be grateful."

I thanked the Lord for our food that we were about to eat and to protect us from the ravages of Mother Nature that was about to hit us.

Everyone ate in silence and helped the caretakers wash and clean up the kitchen. All of the students left to go to their rooms to gather up their things. Neala and I were making small talk with Ms. Flores when the doorbell rang. Standing on the front porch was Father Bayon.

As soon as he made his way into the room, I took his right hand and put it to my forehead.

"Hello, Ali. Do you know anything about this storm that is coming our way?"

"I was called by Mr. Perez from the PAGASA and was told about the storm developing. Chesah and I predicted what it would do before the computers did."

"I bet that is going over big at the weather service."

"I think you're right. They want to talk to us after the storm is over."

Everybody gathered in the classroom. I knew that it wasn't very far to the shelters, maybe one kilometer. A short hike would be what the doctor ordered.

Chesah made her way out of the front door stopping next to

me. "Would you push me there?" she asked.

"I would like that," I said. As soon as we reached the street, little Dalisay reached up to grab my hand. "Can I walk with you?" she asked.

"Oh sure," I said. Chesah saw her with me. "Want to ride in my lap?"

Dalisay became excited. To ride with Chesah was a big thing in her mind. She climbed on board and we made our way towards the shelter.

Standing just outside of the main door was Minda and my parents. I introduced Chesah and Dalisay to them.

"Chesah, do you remember me telling you about Minda? I mentioned her to you when I first came to your home. She is ten-years-old and runs AMN Industries."

Chesah smiled. "I remember. She's a lot like me."

"You two are a lot alike. You're both hard workers and want to excel in life."

We made our way into the shelter heading towards the rear of the building so everyone could get in. My parents found a spot against a wall and sat down. Ms. Flores walked by us. "May we sit with you?" she asked.

"Oh sure. I hope everyone made it here okay?"

"Ms. Flores scanned her group. I think so, but I need to do a roll check just to be sure.

Little Dalisay came up next to me. "Ali, may I sit with you?"

"You sure can." I had moved my things so she could find a place to sit. My mother watched me interact with Dalisay. She smiled as I carried on a conversation with her. We played hand games and we giggled and laughed at each other. After a couple of hours, my parents noticed that Dalisay was becoming sleepy. My mother turned her head towards me. Bring her to me. I picked up Dalisay and put her in my mother's arms.

Minda and I got up to stretch when Father Bayon strolled

by. As soon as he saw Dalisay in my mother's arms, I could see a smile on his face. "Our Lord has his ways of bringing two people together." I looked at my mother. She had her head resting on the top of Dalisay. A wonderful thought hit me.

Minda watched me as I locked my eyes on my mother.

"I know what you're thinking. I saw the same look when Maria was coming out of the shelter with our father."

Minda saw the gleam in my eyes. "It would bring a lot of happiness to our parents. I watched my mother hand Dalisay over to my father so he could hold her for a while. Standing next to him, he rubbed her baby soft hair. "What's her story?" he asked.

"I don't know exactly. She lives at the children's home. She has somehow attached herself to me. I know that she is three-years- old and a wonderful little girl. But other than that, I would have to ask Ms. Flores or Father Bayon.

I watched Dalisay start to open her eyes as she was waking up from her nap. I noticed a little smile on her precious face as she looked up at my father. She then returned her sleepy head to his chest.

Father Bayon had just finished making his way around the room talking to everyone present when he saw my father and Dalisay.

He looked at Minda and me. "I can read the tea leaves that has dropped into your parents' arms." Nothing else said. He clasped his bible against his chest knowing what was happening again to our family.

"Father, may I speak to you alone for a moment."

"Why sure. Let's go over here."

"Ali, what's on your mind these days?"

"Well Father, I mean we would welcome Dalisay into our family, but I have been thinking about this and another person as well."

"Who may that be?"

"I think Chesah would be a great person to add to our family. I know we would have to make some changes in the way we live, but they are not a great concern. Chesah's life is so full of sorrow. She has been turned down by all of her family members. After I got to know her, she only wants a family to love just like everyone else."

"Have you made your feelings known to your parents?"

"Not yet. I wanted to talk to you first."

"Well, I'm always in favor of children being adopted by loving parents. Have you talked to Chesah about this?"

"No. I didn't want to get her hopes up and then have her dreams shattered again by being rejected. That would be an insult to her and hurt her."

"It would at that. Let me nose around a bit and I'll get back to you."

My mother locked eyes on Dalisay, Minda, Father Bayon, and me. She didn't have to say a word. We knew what was going to happen. Dalisay was going to be our new sister. She won't ever have to go without a family to call her own.

Turning away, I looked at the other kids that live in the children's home. They too would love to have a family that they could call home. Seeing Chesah talking to some of the kids, I would love to see her find a family. I bowed my head and said a prayer for her and the others.

Without any notice, I had an idea that may bring a little joy to the people here. I approached Juan, "Would you mind singing some beautiful songs that would bring some joy to everyone?"

At first, he hesitated. "Getting up in front of more than one-hundred people and singing would be a nightmare." He stated.

"It may be. But if you don't ever conquer your fears, they will haunt you for the rest of your life. You will never be able to function as a normal person if your fear is eating you alive."

"I guess I can try," he replied.

"Oh, please do. That would be fantastic."

Seeing Mayor Manalo off to one side talking to Father Bayon, I excused myself for a moment from Juan and approached them.

"Excuse me Mayor and Father, but there is a boy from the children's home who has a wonderful voice. I have asked him if he would sing a few songs for us. He is kinda shy and I think it would help him with his confidence."

Mayor Manalo looked at me. "Who is he?"

"His name is Juan Gonzales."

"Okay. Let's go talk to him and see if we can get Mr. Gonzales to sing for us."

Mayor Manalo turned on the microphone. "Hey everyone. Please be quiet for a moment. I have been told that we have a young man in our midst that has a beautiful voice. And Ali has asked if he would sing something for us. His name is Juan Gonzales."

Juan strolled at a slow pace as he made his way to where the mayor and Father Bayon were standing. Taking the microphone from the mayor, he bowed his head for a moment. All of us heard him say a prayer to our Lord for giving him this chance to prove that he can make it in this world. He looked up at the crowd. I would like to sing, "I Will Follow Him."

His voice began to fill the room with beautiful sounds. After he had finished, the crowd whistled and began cheering him. They have never heard such a beautiful voice like his. He then began to sing "Hallelujah." Then several members from the church choir began to put in the background vocals. The whole room came alive after hearing Juan's voice. The smile on everyone's face told the story of this memorable occasion. He sang several more Christian hymns.

He didn't know it, but this shy young man from the Albay Children's Home was about to become a world-famous singer.

Father Bayon was going to see that his young man got his shot at making something of himself.

Chesah saw little Dalisay with my parents. Standing next to her, I touched her shoulder. She looked up at me.

"I think Dalisay may have some new parents. I'm glad for her. She's a wonderful person."

"I think you may be right." I could see a tear forming in Chesah's eyes. I knew that she wished some family would adopt her and give her the love that she so deserves.

After the entertainment, Mayor Manalo got word from the Emergency Management Coordinator that the storm has passed us by. We can now leave and check on our homes. I saw my parents making their way over to Ms. Flores. They talked for almost fifteen minutes when their meeting finally broke up.

On the way to our house, my mother stayed quiet. Once we had set our things down and I had a pot of coffee brewing in the kitchen, our mother asked Minda and me to sit with her and my father.

"What would you two say if we bring another little girl into our lives?"

Minda didn't have to say a word.

"We would welcome her. I have gotten to know Dalisay since I have been teaching at the children's home. She has her way of pulling on your heart strings. We saw her in your arms. There was a bond being formed between you and her." Father Bayon saw it too and said as much.

I became quiet. My mother looked at me. "Are you two okay with us adopting Dalisay?"

Minda and I smiled at our parents. We both nodded our heads in approval. I wish all of the kids there could have a place that they could call home.

A grand idea popped into my head. "I know of another person in particular that I would love to see someone adopt her.

Her name is Chesah. She's in a wheelchair because of her birth. Her parents have passed on when she was a baby, and the rest of her family has abandoned her because of it. She has never had a real family. She is twelve-years-old, and it hurts me to see her not being wanted by anyone."

Both of my parents knew that I was serious about Chesah.

My father's eyes looked into mine. "I don't think our home could hold another person. If we get Dalisay, she will have to stay in your room."

"I know daddy. We'll just have to move into a bigger home. Something that has at least three bedrooms. And we would have to have the house made accessible for someone in a wheelchair. But these things we can now afford. It would mean a lot to me to have Chesah as a family member as well."

Both of our parents looked at me. "Does she mean that much to you?"

"She does. I talked to Father Bayon about her, and he thinks that it's a wonderful idea. She is a lot alike Minda and me. She loves books. She's intelligent and a hard worker at getting what she wants. But having a family is something she may never have."

Both of our parents looked at each other. My father turned to face me. "This will be a large step in our family adopting two more people. We would have to buy a bigger home or build one with our product." My father hesitated for a moment. "I have no problem with it as long as your mother agrees to it. It's going to take you two to help us with Chesah."

I turned to face Minda. "I have never asked you about your opinion. What would you say if our family grew by two more people?"

Minda just sat there not saying a thing. Then she looked at me and our parents. "I don't have any problems if there is a one-hundred percent agreement. I can definitely see us having to move into a larger home. With four kids and two adults, this place is going to be very small."

My father left us for a moment and headed into the kitchen. Returning to our conversation, he brought everyone a cup of coffee.

"If you make this commitment and your mother says it's a go, then I will start looking for a bigger home or find a place to build one. Then we can start the adoption process."

Everyone locked eyes onto our mother. She had just been put into a spot that she didn't like being put in. "Building a new home would take an awfully long time. If we buy one already built, then we can begin the adoption process for two more girls."

Minda and I became excited at having not one but two more sisters being added to our family. We scurried off to the kitchen. "Let's cook something for dinner to celebrate," I said.

Digging into the freezer and refrigerator, we came up with some pork and the makings for some soup and rice.

Our mother heard all the commotion coming from the kitchen. "What are you two girls up to?"

"We are cooking dinner for tonight."

My mother smiled. "I like that idea. I'll just make my way back to the sofa, pull my shoes off and relax."

She was happy. Our family was about to grow a lot bigger.

# ~Chapter Eighteen~

Chesah observed my parents making their way into Ms. Flores office. She sat in her chair biting her fingernails wondering what the adults were discussing.

I was busy putting some information onto the blackboard when I saw her staring at Ms. Flores office door. I knew what was being said but I didn't want Chesah to know until the right moment. Little did she know, her life was about to be changed forever.

I was finishing up writing a work assignment when Ms. Flores office door opened. She made her way over to where the preschoolers were working in their book.

"Dalisay, would you follow me to my office, please?" Ms. Flores then made her way over to Chesah. "Please come with me to my office for a moment. Ali, would you b come with us as well?"

Chesah looked at me. She didn't know what was going on. She pushed her wheelchair towards Ms. Flores office. Dalisay looked up at me and grabbed my hand.

"Am I in trouble?" she asked.

"Oh no, I don't think so."

We entered Ms. Flores office and found a chair.

"Ali, please shut the door. The reason I have called you, Dalisay and Chesah here is because Mr. and Mrs. Cruz wants to start the adoption process for you two to join Ali and her sister

Minda into their home."

Dalisay jumped out of her chair. She reached for me and gave me a hug.

I saw the tears forming. "Ali, are you adopting me?"

"My parents are. Do you remember them? You met them at the shelter."

"I remember them. They were nice to me. I like them."

I gave her a big smile. "We'll become sisters."

Ms. Flores looked at Chesah. "Do you want to go and become a family member with the Cruz's as well?"

Chesah eyes had teared up as her cheeks reddened. "Do you mean what I think you are saying? Someone wants to adopt me?"

"I do. They want to adopt you and bring you into their home."

Chesah looked at me and smiled. "You had something to do with this."

"You could say that. But also, Father Bayon. He watches over this children's home and when he sees any conceivable way of helping the children, he tries anyway that he can. I asked my parents to bring you into our home and become a sister to Minda, Dalisay and me."

My parents got up from their chair and knelt down next to Chesah. "We would welcome you into our home as our daughter."

Little Dalisay spoke up with a joyful voice. "And me." My parents turned and gave her a hug.

"And you."

I touched Chesah's arm. "Would you like to join us as a family member?" She nodded her head with a 'yes'. I heard her mumbling to herself, '*Somebody wants me to be in their family.*' She covered her face as tears flowed down her red cheeks.

Med and Neala opened Ms. Flores office door. "We couldn't help hearing the news." Med smiled at Chesah and Dalisay. "This is wonderful news." All the other children heard the commotion coming from the office as well. They were all clapping at hearing that Dalisay and Chesah are going to be adopted by Ali's parents.

I faced Ms. Flores. "I think the school knows about what's going on in here." Dalisay stood next to my mother. "Can I call you mommy?"

My mother eyes were red and weeping with joy.

"You sure can."

"When do I get to go home with you?"

"Well, we have to contact the authorities and they have to do some checking. Then we will go to a courthouse and the judge will have to grant us the right to adopt you. It may take several weeks or so."

My mother was trying to say the proper words so a three-year-old may understand what the procedures are.

Chesah knew that this can take months before we could go to court.

I moved in front of everyone. "This delay will give us time to find a bigger home for all of us. Right now, we live in a two-bedroom house. When you and Dalisay come to live with us, we will be in a desperate need of an extra bedroom or two."

"Neala, can you check out a few places that we could go and look at?"

Med did a clearing-of-his-throat kinda sound. "Did you forget something? I'm in the real estate business as well. I have several homes that may work for you."

My parents got up from their chair. "Can we go and look at them? Where are they located? How much are they?" They were firing questions before Med could answer.

"Let me call my secretary. She has the listing of all of my properties." Med made the call and jotted down the information.

"I have seven three-bedroom and two four-bedroom homes for sale. Here's the listing for each property. Go and look at each home and see if there is something that you may like. Call me and I will bring a key so you can go inside and look around. Then we can talk business."

I looked into the faces of my parents. "If we could wait until after school today, Chesah, Dalisay, and I would like to go with you too to look for a new home."

Chesah didn't know what to say. At first, she sat just in her chair staying quiet. "You want me to go with you?"

I smiled at her. "I sure do. You are becoming a family member and that gives you a say into the family business."

Minda smiled. "That's how it was when I became a family member in the Cruz family. We became a team."

I looked at Neala. "Would you take Minda, Chesah and me around to follow our parents in your SUV? Dalisay can ride with them."

Neala smiled. "I don't mind."

"Daddy, can you make me a copy of the addresses that Med gave you? In case we get stuck in traffic."

Neala took the paper my father handed her. Removing her cell phone, she took pictures of the papers. "Where do you want to start?"

My father studied his list. "Let's check out the four-bedrooms first, then we can work our way towards the others."

The first listing was just five blocks away. I could tell that my mother was anxious to get started on our new family project.

Minda, Chesah, Dalisay and I wanted to be in on looking for a new home. This is the first time that I may have to move to another home. Our family seems to be growing at an extraordinary fast pace.

"We still have three hours of school left and Minda can't leave the office until five anyway. Mom, dad, you two go and look at each property on the list. Call me at five p.m . Neala can drive us to your location. If that is okay with you."

Chesah caught the tone in my voice as I spoke to our

parents. After they left, she locked eyes with me. "You don't sound anything like a nine-year-old girl. If I were to shut my eyes, I would have thought that there were just adults talking to each other."

I kinda made some giggling noises at what she just told me. "I know what you mean. I have been told that a lot. Especially when I was getting AMN Industries started. Every adult took a second glance at me. I was only four when all this began."

The last three hours were the slowest time I think that I have ever encountered. Med made a call to his secretary and asked for her to bring all the keys for the listings that she provided. At a quarter to five, there was a knock on the classroom door. Med left the room for a few minutes to see who it was, and upon his return, he dangled a large key ring at us.

"Ali, here are the keys to all of the houses that you have on your list. If you find something your family likes, call me and I'll give your parents the price."

"Okay. Thank you Med, for helping us out with this project."

"You're welcome. Your family has taken on quite a challenge and I like it."

"Med, have you ever thought about adopting someone yourself? It's a rewarding feeling that you can only imagine by helping a person that has no family or home to go to."

"I have never thought about it that much. I'm always so busy."

I lowered my head. I didn't say another word about this subject. The tone in his voice said it all.

My parents pulled their SUV into the driveway of the children's home a little after five p.m. Little Dalisay peered out the window. When she saw her new parents, she ran out of the building smiling and laughing as they were walking towards her. My mother bent down and scooped her up into her arms. We walked out to where they had stopped on the sidewalk leading towards the front door. Looking back at the windows of the children's home, I could see the faces of every young person there staring at us. My heart felt saddened for the other children. They too would have loved to have someone adopt them and to have the growing love that was taking place before their own eyes. I bent my head down to say a short prayer, *"Dear Lord, I want to help those who need parents in their lives."*

"Ali, are you about ready to go?" a voice called out to me.

I looked at where the voice was coming from. It was Neala.

"Oh sure. I was just thinking."

"We heard you. And that was a nice thought." Neala looked at what had caught my attention was all of the faces that starred at us.

As soon as we had Neala's SUV loaded, we made our way to find us a new home.

The first house that was on the list seemed no bigger than what we already have. The builder just made the rooms a lot smaller and called it a four-bedroom.

Scratch this one off the list. Chesah took out a pen and marked it out. She made notes next to the property.

I saw what she was doing. "Good thinking," I told her.

She smiled at my gesture.

The next one on our list was more to our liking.

"Now this one is more like it," as I gazed at the size of each room. The bedrooms were big enough for two people to sleep in and have some room to move around. The largest room, besides the master bedroom, would be big enough for Chesah to move her chair around to make herself comfortable. She smiled. "I like it. I know that I'm going to have to get used to having another person in the same room, but I'll manage." Minda and I both liked her answer. "Sometimes we have to make sacrifices in order to help others." We headed to where our parents were having a conversation with Neala. The three of us spoke at the same time. "We like it here."

I looked at Dalisay. "Do you like this home?"

"I do, Ali. It's big and wonderful."

My parents looked at the faces of us four children. They knew that this home would be satisfactory to raise us in.

My father looked at Chesah. "If we buy this home, I will have a ramp put in the front and the back for you. If there is anything else that you may need to make yourself comfortable, let me know and I will see to it."

"You have done so much already for me. I don't want to be a bother to you."

My mother knelt down next to Chesah's chair. "You're not a bother to us. We'll do whatever it takes to make you comfortable to be with this family." Everyone of us moved around Chesah and her chair. Resting our hands on hers, my mother looked straight into Chesah's eyes. "You are a blessing that our Lord has given us. All of us knew that we must make some adjustments when Ali asked us to adopt you into our family, and we accepted that." I saw little Dalisay holding Chesah hands, "I want to help too." Chesah had tears forming. She knew that this family was what life is meant to be. "Love." Her dreams had finally come true.

# ~Chapter Nineteen~

Our parents and Med came to an agreement on the purchase of this four-bedroom home for our new family. After the transfer of deed and the signing of all of the papers, Minda and I began our task of packing all of our belongings into boxes and putting them in the front room. We helped our mother in the kitchen with boxing up everything except the kitchen sink. While we were busy packing up, Med sent a crew of painters and cleaners over to our new home to make it bright and fresh as possible. As soon as we had everything ready to move, my father hired a moving company to load a large truck of all of our things.

The look on Neala's face told me that she was excited to see our family grow. She now had several more children to help raise as a so-called stepmother. Even though she was not related to us, I have grown extremely attached to her in these last five years.

\*\*\*\*\*

The five of us kept watching the school's clock. I caught Neala looking at her watch several times. She wanted to go to our new home as much as we did. As soon as school was over, we piled into Neala's SUV and we're happily on our way. Neala and our parents set the dining room table watching us girls to see how we were going to handle our newest problem. The three of us were a lot older than Dalisay. Would we push her off to the side and put her into whatever room we wanted her in, or would we just let her decide for herself? After our parents claimed the master bedroom for themselves, which is rightfully so, the other three bedrooms were up for grabs. We four girls now had a dilemma to solve. Someone was going to have a roommate.

I gathered all the girls together. "Okay, here is what we must do. We either flip a coin for the rooms or draw straws. The shortest straw gets to claim a room first. The person left out can choose whomever they want to room in with."

"Can we all agree on it?" There was a unanimous decision. "We will flip for it."

Dalisay didn't know what to say. She never had to flip or draw anything before.

"So, in order to make this fair, we'll have momma do the flipping and she will decide who is against who."

Little Dalisay made her way over to our mother.

"Momma, can you help us? We must choose a room and we need your help."

I caught the look on our mother's face as she melted at hearing Dalisay's soft childlike voice. After our family's devastating loss of Maria, Dalisay brought a new light to all of us.

My mother liked the idea that we girls have asked her to be a part of our decision.

Minda pulled a coin out of her pocket.

Our mother looked at each of us. "Minda, you'll challenge Ali and Chesah you'll challenge Dalisay. Then the losers will challenge each other. The last person can choose whomever they want to stay with. Are we in agreement with this new rule of the house?"

Everyone agreed.

"Chesah, you and 'Dalisay will go first. Dalisay, do you want heads or tails?"

"Heads," she said with jubilation in her voice.

My mother took the coin and flipped it into the air letting it land on the floor and the five of us gathered around. It was tails.

My mother bent over and picked it up. "Chesah, you get to choose which room you want."

Knowing that it was the largest of the three. "I'll take the room to the right of the bathroom."

"Now Ali, you choose what side of the coin you want."

"I'll take tails."

Our mother's voice seemed to have a little excitement in it. "Okay then. Let the game begin." I could tell that our mother was getting into this game of chance. She flipped the small coin into the air. We all watched as it rolled around several times before it fell flat, landing on heads.

Momma looked at Minda. "You can now choose which room you want."

"I'll take the other room on the other side to the bathroom."

My mother picked up the coin again. "Now Dalisay, you and Ali will compete against each other."

Dalisay looked at me. I saw a beautiful smile on her face.

"Ali, are you ready to compete against me?"

"I sure am. You call it," I said.

Dalisay, raised her voice. "Heads."

Momma tossed the coin into the air. It hit the floor and rolled all the way across our living area to the opposite wall. It landed on heads.

Dalisay picked up the coin and gave it back to Minda.

"Thanks, Minda, for the use of your coin."

I watched Minda's face. Reading the emotions that were beginning to show, she was beginning to have feelings for little Dalisay as well.

Momma touched Dalisay's shoulder. "You now have the other room. And Ali, you get to choose whom you want to room with."

I have always had a kind heart for others. "To make this fair, let's draw straws. Give a different straw length to Minda, Chesah, and Dalisay. Momma you hold them, and I will pick one. The person who has the longest straw, I will have to room with."

Our mother cut a straw into three different lengths. She then gave each room holder a straw. She then had each person put their straw into a paper bag. She shook it up several times, held it high in the air so no one could peek, then she opened it.

"Ali, reach in and grab one straw." I reached for a straw and pulled it up. It belonged to Dalisay.

My mother knelt down to her. "Are you okay having Ali room with you?" She looked up at me, then she took my hand.

"I was hoping that Ali would stay in the room with me. I dreamed that one day she would adopt me, and my wish came true. Now I get to stay in the same room as her."

Her soft voice and her precious words melted my heart. I became a total mess. My mother saw my face and the redness in my eyes. Dalisay's whole life has been in the children's home. She was left on the front steps of the home in a small basket with a note. *"She should have never been brought into this world. Please take care of her."*

I knelt in front of her. "I would love to stay in the same room as you."

Dalisay smiled at me and gave me a big hug. She whispered in my ear, "I love you, Ali."

Pulling back, I looked at her face. "I love you too, Dalisay."

As the movers began to bring in our boxes, all of us pitched in to put them in the proper places. After the last box was delivered, our family now had the chore of putting our new home together.

"I think I'm going to miss our old home. Someday, someone else will live there. I have so many memories that have taken place here."

"Daddy, are we going to sell our old home?"

"I already have. I made a deal with Med. I used the old place as a down payment on this one. He now owns it."

"Oh, I didn't know that a deal was made. I'll miss the old place. Our lives changed forever in that home."

My father stood next to me putting his arm on my shoulder. "It did at that. The past is now memories that cannot be changed. Now we have a new place to live and new family members. We'll make new memories here. Memories that will last a lifetime."

I knew that he was right.

Strolling into Chesah's new room, I saw her staring at the bare walls. "What's up?" I asked.

Chesah looked over at me. "These last couple of weeks, my world that I use to know is now turned upside down since I met you. Now I'm in a home with a real family. I took part in a challenge with the government weather people and I also helped with teaching others. It's like I use to sit on the sidelines of a soccer game, but now, I'm on the field running and playing the game."

"I know what you mean. I discovered that I too was adopted. I taught myself to read and understand books at the age of four. I didn't know why, but Father Bayon was the person who brought my gift to life. Our family had to make adjustments every day to things that kept changing. I knew from that day on, my life would never be the same again. So far, I have built a company and hired hundreds of workers, paying them a better wage than anywhere else. Made a product to help save lives from typhoons and have started teaching students. I've had death stare me in the face on more than one occasion and I'm only nine-years-old. But I also knew that our Lord would lead me down the path that he wants me to take. I truly believe that he wants me to reach out and help as many people as I can."

Chesah knew deep down in her soul where I was coming

from. Our worlds are different, but yet, we're still the same.

# ~Chapter Twenty~

Working at a pace from eight in the morning until five in the evening, time just seemed to fly by. Med and I were putting a lot of information into these students' brains. On Friday, November tenth, the three musketeers were standing on the front steps of the children's home. Ms. Flores smiled at us as we entered the building.

"Ali, I have some great news. I just got off of the phone with the adoption agency. Your parents were approved with the adoptions. I'll call your father now and let him know. The court date is next week."

Med smiled at me. "Congratulations on helping with the adoption. Dalisay and Chesah will be very happy to hear the great news."

"Med, I would like to personally thank you for helping my family in finding a bigger home. You are a very special person in my life. No words can be said about your generosity to helping others."

Med looked down at me. "My father has always taught me that a little kindness goes a long way. If you give a little of yourself to others, it will come back to you ten-fold."

Med and I watched as the students made their way into the classroom. I waited to see Dalisay and Chesah come in.

Ms. Flores walked over to Dalisay and asked her to come into her office for a moment. I noticed that Chesah never made it into the classroom. She was absent.

"Ali, could you check on Chesah?"

"I sure can," I said as I left the room. A young boy watched me. "She never left her room," he said.

Heading to her room, my thoughts on how to tell her was scrambling in my brain.

I gave her door a light knock. Then I did it again.

I heard her voice. "It's open."

"Are you coming to class?" I asked.

She had her back turned towards me. "I will be there in a minute."

I could hear her voice had a muffle sound to it. She was crying.

"Are you okay?" I asked.

"I'm okay. I never really thought about being someone who is going to have a real family before. My whole life, I have gotten use to knowing that I will never leave this place."

"Well, I am personally informing you that the adoption will happen. Ms. Flores just told me as soon as I entered the building. The court date is next week."

Chesah looked at me. "Thanks for being here. You have touched my life so much. I don't know how I can ever repay you."

"You don't owe me a thing. I saw something in you that touched my heart. I told my parents about you and they could see that you are a very special person. Our parents cannot have children of their own. That's why they have adopted Minda and me. And since our father is the president of AMN Industries, our parents are now financially able to grow our family even larger."

"Are you ready to go to class now?"

Chesah looked up at me. "Yeah, I am."

\*\*\*\*\*

On the way towards the classroom, my cell phone rang. It was Mr. Perez, the Director of the PAGASA Weather Service.

"Ali, can you and your friend Chesah come to our offices tomorrow? We would like to talk to you and her about your future plans. I can have a plane waiting for you at the airport in Legaspi City if you can make it."

"Let me ask Chesah?"

Putting my phone on hold, I looked towards her. "Mr. Perez wants us to come to his office in Queson City tomorrow. Are you up to making a trip?"

Chesah smiled. "They want me?" was all she said.

"They do. They want to talk to both of us."

"I'm game." She let out with such a joyous voice.

I took my phone off of hold. "We can be there. What time do we need to be at the airport?"

"I'll have a plane waiting for you at eight-thirty tomorrow morning."

"Mr. Perez. I need to let you know that Chesah is in a wheelchair."

"I see," he replied. "Thanks for the heads up. I'll have to let the flight and ground crew know so they can accommodate her."

As soon as we entered the classroom, I found Neala in Ms. Flores office.

"Neala, I just got off of the phone with Mr. Perez. He wants to see Chesah and me in his office tomorrow morning. He'll have a plane waiting for us at eight-thirty a.m. at Legaspi City Airport."

"Are you okay with this?" I asked.

Neala felt a little giddiest. "Let me check my schedule."

She acted like she was looking at an invisible book.

"I'm free," she replied.

Ms. Flores looked towards me. "I'll have to check with the administrators on letting Chesah make a trip with you."

"The PAGASA Weather Service is where we'll be going to in Queson City," I said.

Ms. Flores shuffled some papers on her desk. "I'll make some calls and let you know by this afternoon."

Chesah just sat in her chair without saying a word. She then looked up at my face.

I smiled at her. "Ms. Flores has to check with the children's home administrative people on letting you go on a trip with me. After next week this won't be a problem for us anymore."

Med and I started working on our school lessons. After breaking for lunch, Ms. Flores called me into her office.

"Ali, I was given permission to let Chesah travel with you. When will you two be returning?"

"We should be back by the evening time. If there are any problems, I will call you and let you know."

"Thanks. That will be okay. I have to let the administrators know of any changes."

"I understand."

Searching for Chesah I found her at the lunch table. I whispered in her ear. "It's a go."

Returning to the classroom after lunch, I made the announcement. "Med will be teaching the class tomorrow. Chesah and I have been asked to attend a meeting at the PAGASA Weather Service in Queson City. We should be back tomorrow night."

A young girl asked, "Why do they want to talk to Chesah?"

"Remember when I let you see my computer and we talked about the typhoon? Chesah's answer has caught the attention of their upper management. Now they want to talk to her and me about how we came about making our prediction on this storm. They are sending a plane to pick us up at the airport in the morning. When we return, we'll have a discussion in class on what we talked about and about how important it is to have the most accurate weather reports possible. This will be a great way to learn about our planet and how the weather plays a very important part of life around the world."

"Neala, what time shall we pick up Chesah?"

"Let's make it seven-thirty. That will give us some lead time at the airport."

"Chesah, are you sure you're up to making this trip?"

"Oh yeah," she happily replied.

"Okay then. We'll be here at seven-thirty." I left the room for a few minutes so I could tell Ms. Flores our plans.

*****

Returning to the classroom, I needed to get back on track of teaching my students. I saw Med was going over medical issues with his class.

"Okay everyone. Let's get back to working on our class assignments." After going around observing each of my students, and answering their questions, I knew which ones were capable of moving up the ladder on their education. Out of the twenty-five students that I worked with, I had seven that were outstanding. Pulling each one aside, I asked them if they would like to push their education to the next level. All seven agreed. What they were learning was not a challenge.

Grabbing college books on every subject that I purchased, I passed them around.

"I want you seven to start working out of these books." As they skimmed through them, I heard a girl make a gulping sound.

"This will challenge you to push yourself beyond what most other students study. These books will make you think about how to solve a problem. Excuse me for a moment." I left the room so

I could get a white board from the storage room.

"You can work as a team on problem solving and explain how you came up with your answer. I will check your work and test you on it."

"Now let's start on working on some problems." I wrote several problems on the white board. "Open your science book. Read chapters four and five. I'll check on your progress later."

Ms. Flores watched me as I had pulled the seven students from the rest of the group. Strolling over to where I was working with the rest of the class, she had a curious look on her face.

"Why are they working out of different books?"

I turned to face her. "They are exceptional students. I spotted it when they were working on the problems the others were working on. So, I challenged them to push themselves to the next level."

"I see," Ms. Flores replied. I want to see their grades after a six-week period."

"I will show you everything as they progress."

Ms. Flores left the classroom and headed back to her office.

Turning to face Med. "Are you going to be okay with me leaving tomorrow morning?"

"I'll have to deal with working with the youngsters, but I think I can manage for a day."

"Thanks Med."

*****

Standing in front of a large turboprop aircraft, Chesah looked up at the shiny white behemoth.

"I never been this close to an airplane before," she said.

I looked over at her. "Once we get inside, you can look around." She smiled so brightly with her big white teeth.

A ground crew walked over to where we were standing.

"Are you ladies ready to board?"

"We are," I said.

A special lift was brought over to us. Chesah, Neala, and I got on and we were lifted up to the entrance doorway. Chesah maneuvered her chair into the middle aisle.

Looking over her right shoulder, she spotted Neala.

"Neala, can I get a window seat? I want to watch the world go by."

"Oh sure. Let me put my things in the overhead bin and I'll help you."

Neala picked up Chesah and put her into a window seat. She looked up at Neala's face. "Thanks."

"You're welcome," Neala responded.

I moved to the seat next to her. "What do you think so far?"

"We'll, I'm anxious to get into the air."

Our flight was an hour and fifty minutes before the wheels touched the earth. Our plane was taxied over to a special hanger that is used by the PAGASA department. The same kind of lift was brought over to the exit door just like before. Once we were all seated into a large van, we made our way to through Manila and onward to Queson City. I could see Chesah's eyes were extremely large as she tried to soak into her brain as much as she could of all the images that flashed before her.

She let out a low mumble, "There are so many people." Jeepney's, motorbikes and almost any other form of transportation that could carry a person rolled past us.

Pulling into driveway of the PAGASA Office, we were escorted into the front waiting room. We filled out the questionnaire and had our photo taken for an ID Badge. Chesah felt like she was a million dollars. I looked at Neala's face and she smiled at me. "Bringing Chesah was a great idea, she'll remember this for the rest of her life."

"I agree."

Mr. Perez stepped into the waiting room where we were

seated. "Hello Ali, Neala." Looking over at the girl in the wheelchair, "You must be Chesah."

"I am," she said.

"It's so nice to meet you. The email I received from Ali stated that you are quite a remarkable young lady. I understand the information I sent to Ali about the weather disturbance was handed off to you for your input. "

"Ali asked me to take a look at the information and give her my idea of what I was looking at."

"Well, your information was correct."

Chesah put on her serious face, "I have to make a confession, Ali helped me with some of it."

"I see."

"May I ask how old you are? And where did you get your education?"

"I'm twelve, and I've been studying science books since I waa able to read. I like to study anything that pertains to science or the universe."

"I can see why Ali was surprised when you two met. You are a lot like her. Let's go into the computer room where we monitor the weather around the world."

The look on Chesah's face as she witnessed all of the television screens flashing different weather patterns that were effecting the globe, told us what we knew all along. I do believe that she may one day work here or a place like this one.

"What do you think?" I asked.

She looked up at me, "I like this a lot."

She turned her chair towards Mr. Perez. "May I see the satellite images of the Philippines?"

Mr. Perez asked an assistant to bring up the latest image that was available.

Chesah locked her eyes onto the screen. We watched her emotions that reflected off of her face as she scanned the screen, was intense. Chesah was connecting her mind to the weather that was happening right now. Mr. Perez became fascinated at watching her. After several minutes of silence, everybody wanted to know what was going through her mind.

"Chesah, what do you see when you look at these satellite images?"

My words brought her back to all of us in the room.

"Sorry, my mind became part of the images. It's as though I could feel the air currents and temperature of the atmosphere."

I knew what Chesah was feeling. I too, have had those kinds of thoughts.

Chesah repositioned herself in her chair. She pointed at a television screen on the wall. "There's a tropical wave coming off the coast of Guam."

Mr. Perez looked at what she was talking about. "Chesah, please come over to this terminal. You can use the pointer to show us what you are seeing."

Chesah rolled her wheelchair over to where a young man was sitting.

"May I?" she asked him. He got up from his chair and moved it aside. She took his mouse and pointed at the disturbed weather that had caught her attention. "This will be our next typhoon. With the high pressure building over the southern Philippines and the low over the northern section, Luzon will be hit within the next seventy-two hours."

The whole office staff locked eyes onto what this young girl, sitting in a wheelchair, was describing. It seems as though she doesn't know what she's talking about. Some just shook their heads mumbling at a low tone.

Mr. Perez became intrigued on how Chesah came up with her hypnosis.

"Care to explain your prediction."

Chesah sat quiet for a moment. "Well for starters, the water temperature running through the Philippine Sea is at thirty-one degree Celsius. The upper atmosphere is at a minus forty degree

Celsius according to the information being shown to us. That is what started the disturbed weather off the coast of Guam. With the wind currents moving east to west at forty-one kilometers per hour, this wave will move into the Philippine Sea. The high pressure just south of Japan and north of Palau will force it into the low pressure that is sitting between the two high pressure areas. That's how I see what is about to happen."

Mr. Perez seemed impressed with Chesah. "Your input makes for us a very probable problem to work. Thanks."

Chesah smiled. "Your welcome."

"Chesah, what grade are you currently in?"

"I'm going into the eighth."

"I see," Mr. Perez said. "Are you going to go to college when you graduate from high school?"

"I hope so. But, it's very expensive."

I stepped into this conversation. "I'll make sure that Chesah gets the best education. She may be out of college before she turns sixteen."

Chesah gave me the strangest look.

"Say what?" she replied.

Mr. Perez seemed interested now. "Just how are you going to pull this off," he asked.

Neala smiled and stayed quite. 'They don't know me and how I can teach. If Chesah wants a college degree then that goal is possible.'

"Well, if Chesah would like to work here or someplace else, I can give her the education that will make her stand out in front of anyone."

Mr. Perez just took the bait. "A challenge?" he commented, "If Chesah can graduate from any university in the country before she turns sixteen, I will give her a job here. And I'll guarantee it in writing."

I thought for a moment. "I like it."

Facing Chesah, "Are you up for a monumental challenge?"

She sat quite for several seconds. "I have never backed down from a challenge yet!"

My eyes widened, "Oh my." I said as I put my hand up to my mouth. "You sound just like me."

Neala stepped over to Chesah and knelt in front of her, "I have heard those exact same words coming from Ali. You are about to embark on a journey that no one can ever take from you."

Mr. Perez smiled. "I like it. I'm witnessing a challenge being made with my very own eyes" Chesah, this challenge gives you roughly three years to complete. Are you up to it?"

Chesah smiled back "I am."

On the return flight home, Chesah seemed quiet. I moved next to her. She kept staring out the window at the clouds that drifted by.

"What are you thinking about?" I asked.

"Oh, how am I going to pull off this challenge?"

"We are going to do it the same way Minda did. She got a college degree at the age of nine."

Chesah turned and smiled at me. "Thanks Ali, for wanting to help me."

After our plane had landed at Legaspi Airport, we made our way to the children's home.

As soon as we entered the main building, we found Ms. Flores in her office working.

She looked up from the papers on her desk. "Hey everyone. How did your trip go today?"

Chesah smiled. "Everything went well. I was offered a job there as soon as I graduate from college."

"That's fantastic," Ms. Flores said.

"I was also challenged to receive this college diploma by the age of sixteen."

"Oh my. That is a challenge."

I looked at them. "It will be for sure, but it's possible."

Neala and I left the children's home and headed towards our new home.

\*\*\*\*\*

Heading up the front steps, I could see the new ramp was just about finished. Opening the front door I saw my parents and Minda sitting down to dinner.

"Hello everybody."

My mother looked up from her plate. "Wash your hands and sit down for dinner."

"Neala, would you like to join us?" I asked.

"I'd love too," she said.

While enjoying a home cooked meal, I brought up the challenge that Chesah and I have taken on.

My father looked at me, "Can you make this happen with Chesah in that short of time?"

"I know I can," I said.

My mother smiled, "I know you can too. I've seen it myself how you worked with Minda."

The next morning Neala and I arrived with Med on the front porch of the classroom at the same time. "Good morning Med. How did it go working with the whole class yesterday?"

"Well, I got along just fine with all of the students. Working with the preschoolers brought back a lot of memories of when I was a small boy. You know, the four-year-old boy named Alberto seemed to like me working with him on his spelling and numbers. I was surprised to hear him as he tried to read a sentence I wrote for him."

I glanced at Med. "I think he'll be someone to work with. He seems to show a lot of determination to better himself."

Med looked over at him. "He does at that."

After a two hour class, a young boy strolled over to where I was standing. "Ms. Flores wants to speak to you in her office."

"Okay, thanks." Putting down the marker. "Class, I'll be right back. I have to see Ms. Flores."

Upon entering her office, she looked up from her desk.

"Ali, I just got off of the phone with the children's home administrators. You have a court date on June tenth at nine a.m."

"That's Chesah's birthday. How wonderful. That will be the best birthday she will always remember."

Ms. Flores smiled. "I believe you're right. She'll never forget the day she became officially adopted by her new parents."

I could see a few tears starting to form. She sniffled a few times, taking a tissue to wipe her face. "It gives me great joy to see these children having a chance for a better life."

"I think you'll be proud of what she will do with her life. At the PAGASA Office, everyone there stopped working so they could hear her speak. Her presence commanded their attention. We'll know if what she said in a couple of days, pans out. If it does, she'll be someone they may turn to. Not bad for a twelve -year-old girl from a children's home."

Returning to the classroom, I found Chesah was in a deep discussion with another boy. They were expressing their differences of opinions on the climate change that we're witnessing on this planet.

"Ali, can you help us?" Chesah asked.

"What do you want to know?"

"We are discussing climate change. And we're at differences in opinions."

"Well, you know the earth's climate is always changing. It has done this many times in the last several hundred-million years. By its moving, the earths liquid iron core may switch poles like it has done before. This disruption that surrounds our planet can and will cause all kinds of problems with our climate. There are debates going on as we speak about how humans are causing these problems. Now do some research on this subject and let's discuss it. Heres some fuel for thought, 'When did the

last climate change make a significant change in our climate?'
Think about it. One that comes to mind is the ice age."

# ~Chapter Twenty-One~

For the last month, time seemed to just float by us. Now we are sitting in the courtroom with Chesah and Dalisay. Standing up, I saw Med and Ms. Flores walk in. I waved at them as they found a place to sit.

Minda grabbed my hand. "This is so exciting. We are about to have two more sisters."

"I know. This is so cool," I said.

At a little past nine a.m., the courtroom judge walked in. Everyone stood up as he approached the bench. All except Chesah. He saw her sitting in her wheelchair, and he smiled at her as he seated himself.

The judge called our case. "The parties involved with the adoption of Chesah Bolling and Dalisay Rivero, please stand."

My parents and Ms. Flores stood up.

"Are the children here and present at these proceedings."

Chesah rolled her chair next to where Dalisay was standing. The judge looked at both of them.

"Are you willing to be adopted by the Cruz family?"

Chesah looked at Dalisay. "We are."

"Then I will grant this adoption as being final. You are now part of the Cruz family."

I stood next to both of my new sisters. "Happy birthday Chesah. This will be one birthday that you will never forget."

Chesah looked up at me and I could see tears in her eyes. "I never thought it was possible for me to have a real family."

Father Bayon made his way over to where we were standing.

"Hello, Father," I said taking his right hand and putting it to my forehead.

"Hello, Ali. I see that you have created and surpassed another milestone. One day, your footprints in the sand will have many followers."

I looked up and smiled and I knew those words would be with me for the rest of my life. I watched little Dalisay run over to our parents. My mother bent down so she could wrap her arms around Dalisay. I watched my father bend down next to them as well. Minda touched my shoulder. "Now it's official. We are a family of six."

I looked at her. "We have always known that our family will never stay the same. Our parents have always reached out to help others."

Minda smiled at me. "I know that's right."

Our parents stood up next to our new sisters. "Are you girls ready to go to your new home?"

They looked at each other, then up at our parents.

"We are."

Neala walked over to where we were all standing.

My father turned to face her. "Neala, can you take Ali and Minda home? I want to go to the children's home and help our newest family members gather up their things."

Neala smiled. "Sure can. If you need any help, just call."

Sitting in Neala's SUV, she looked at me as we were leaving the courthouse.

"Well, what are your thoughts on having new sisters."

"It's great," I said.

Minda twirled her fingers through her hair as she stared out the car window. Turning in my seat, I could tell that there was something bothering her.

As soon as we pulled up to the front of our new home, Minda got out of the car and never said a word to us.

Neala caught on to what just happened. "I think Minda needs a sister-to-sister talk. She feels left out of your life now that you are teaching at the children's home and you helped your parents adopt two more sisters."

I knew where Neala was coming from. The human emotions that we all possess has kicked in making Minda to feel left out.

I waited for a half-an-hour before I knocked on Minda's bedroom door. Seeing her lying on her bed, I could hear her sobbing. I sat next to her. "Hey girlfriend, what's with all of those tears?" At first, she didn't say a word. She then rolled over so she could see me.

"I'm not part of this family anymore," she said.

"Who told you that? Just because we have two more sisters in our home doesn't make you less of one of us. You and I will always be sisters and best friends. Our lives have changed so much in these four years and it will never stop changing. We just have to change with it as time moves forward. Now that we have Chesah with us, you'll see that she is very intelligent, just like you. If we can help her with her studies, I think she can have a college degree at a very early age. She has already been asked to join the PAGASA when she turns sixteen. If you help me with Chesah and Dalisay, they too will be able one day, to help our nation and fellow Filipinos." Those simple words were what Minda wanted to hear, that she is needed and loved.

Neala had just put a pot of coffee on when the front door opened. Chesah rolled in with a lap full of stuff.

Watching Dalisay walk in with her arms full of her things, I got a giggle watching her trying to balance her few books and papers along with some clothes. She was trying to walk with her tongue sticking out. She then said, "I got this. I got this," and then they all hit the floor. "I don't got this." Neala, Minda and I laughed at her demeanor. The three of us helped her pick up her things, taking them to her room. My father strolled in with arms full of Chesah's books.

"Anymore?" I asked.

"Yeah, lots more," my father said gritting his teeth.

We made our way outside to the back of our SUV. There were still lots of books, clothes, and personal items that needed to be taken in.

With our arms full of things, we made our way to their rooms. I had just sat the last of Chesah's clothes down when my phone rang. It was Mr. Perez with PAGASA.

"Ali, are you with Chesah?"

"I am. She has officially become my new sister today. We are moving her things in our new home as we speak."

"Can you put your phone on speaker? She needs to hear what I have to say."

Covering my phone against my chest, I yelled at Chesah to come to the front room.

"What's up?" she asked.

"Mr. Perez is on my phone. He wants you to hear what he has to say."

"Chesah, the prediction that you came up with is correct. The weather disturbance just west of Guam is now a cyclone and is moving towards the Philippines at thirty kilometers per hour. We are expecting it to hit here in the next thirty-six to forty-eight hours.

Looking at Chesah's face, I knew what she just heard gave her a lot to think about.

Chesah stared at my phone. "Can you upload the data to Ali's email? I want to know everything. Maybe I can come up with something else that may help you, like where it might hit, and how big will it grow? Etc."

"I'll send you what we have. When I receive your input, I'll compare it with the information that our people have put together here. Then we can make an announcement."

"Okay. Thanks," Chesah said.

We continued helping Chesah and Dalisay put their things away when I received an email alert on my phone. Seeing the large map on the cellphone was a pain. Retrieving my laptop, I set it up using my phone as a hot-spot. "Until we can get the internet connected here, this will have to do for now."

Setting the laptop on our dining table, Neala and the rest of us sat back and watched Chesah study the information contained in the email.

My father asked in a low voice. "Who wants coffee?" Everyone except Dalisay raised their hand. Even Chesah looked up from her work and said. "I do."

I think my mother is going to have to buy a bigger coffee pot. Ours won't make enough for just one go around.

Dalisay looked at me. "I have never tasted coffee before. What does it taste like?" she asked.

"It's bitter and served hot. Some folks like it black and others with sugar and milk."

"I'll have to try it," she said smiling at me.

Chesah studied the information for almost fifteen minutes.

"May I?" looking at her.

"Oh, sure," she replied.

I studied everything that I had received on my laptop screen. Looking at Chesah. "What do you think?"

She stared straight ahead, then she turned her head to look me in my eyes. "This storm will stall out in the Philippine Sea for another day. It will then continue to build up strength as it moves towards Mindanao. There it will move along the coastline heading upwards towards the Visayas Islands. If the low-pressure area that will be sitting over Sorsogon stays, the high-pressure area behind this storm will push it in there."

I looked at Chesah's face. "I believe that you are right in your presumption. Send a reply to Mr. Perez with what we just discussed." While we are discussing things," I turned to face our mom and dad, "I think Chesah needs to have her own cell phone and laptop. She will be getting more of these kind of questions from PAGASA in the future."

My mother looked puzzled. "Why would this government weather organization keep asking Chesah about weather conditions? Don't they have their own meteorologist on their payroll?"

"They do. But I think it has to do with looking into the future. They're always looking for personnel that have a brilliant mind and a desire to study the weather. Someone who does not need years of going to college to predict what the weather may do. Chesah seems to have caught the attention of their director. Her predictions have been remarkably accurate, and she is now just thirteen. They have already made her an offer to work there after she finishes her education. That is something that just doesn't happen to just anybody."

My father smiled at me. "You're correct. In the real world, jobs like that are hard to come by. They only seek out the best of the best. If Chesah can help them in predicting the weather more accurately, then it will help our country and the people here."

I caught the look on Chesah's face. Her life has taken a turn to what our Lord had in mind for her. She no longer feels left out or not wanted in this world. Her life has a purpose to help others, the same way I feel about myself.

After Chesah replied to the email, we watched our mother walk out of the kitchen with a birthday cake for Chesah.

"Happy birthday, Chesah," she said.

Chesah's face lit up with excitement.

"For me? I've never had a birthday cake before."

I caught sight of tears forming in her eyes.

"No one has ever given me a birthday party with cake. Now I have a new family, a new home and a new life." I stood next to her and hugged her neck. Then our whole family stood around her and gave her a family hug.

Minda reached out and held Chesah's hand. "We are a close family. We share in our happiness and our pain. We help each other as well as others. That's how we became this wonderful family."

Little Dalisay looked up at us. "And me."

"Especially you," I said, smiling at her.

She smiled back and giggled.

I knelt down next to her and giggled with her. "It feels good to laugh," I said.

# ~Chapter Twenty-Two~

Opening the door to the classroom, we could hear someone trying to play the piano. Med looked at me as we sat our things down. Opening the music room door, we took notice of a little girl with a deformed right arm trying to play. Med made some noises so our presence would not surprise her. She turned in her seat and seeing us staring at her, she got up.

I was smiling at her. "Oh, please don't stop on a count of us. We heard music being played as we entered the building". She slowly returned to the piano bench. "I didn't think anybody could hear me trying to play."

I saw the look on Med's face. She had touched his heart. "Oh, we like the fact that someone is wanting to play on the piano and maybe wanting to learn. I don't want to seem rude, but we don't know your name."

"It's Ana," she replied.

Med stood next to her, "Ana, may I help you with learning to play the piano? I taught a young man several years back that had a similar problem with his left arm."

She tried to cover up her handicap. Med knew what to do. "Oh, don't cover up your arm. Let's make good use out of it and make some beautiful music together. Ok?"

I could see a small smile on her face.

"Someday, I wish that were possible that I could play the piano."

Med smiled at her. "It's very possible, if you practice. Can you show me what you do know?"

She placed her left hand on the keyboard and then her right arm. I noticed that she only had small nubs as fingers attached to her lower arm.

Med studied her motions. "Okay, let's try this." He moved her right arm so she could touch the keys with less effort. She struggled at first with this new challenge, but after several minutes she was playing better than before.

"Now, practice playing like this and you will hear an improvement in the sound quality of your music." She thanked Med for helping her with her challenge.

Returning to the classroom, Med and I watched as the students began to wander in.

Juan looked at Med and I. "We heard someone playing the piano. Ana seemed to shrivel up when Juan spoke."

"Yes, Ana was. She wants to learn to play." I could hear several of the kids making mockery gestures because of her birth defect.

I saw a girl of about ten years of age making bad body gestures. Standing in front of her, I pointed my finger. "What do you do?"

She didn't answer.

"Do you play a musical instrument? Do you play sports? What makes you so much better than the rest of us?"

She still didn't answer.

I looked at the entire room of people. "Please don't hurt others feelings by making fun of them. That's just being cruel and mean. No good can come from it."

She looked at the others who stood around her then she stared at me. "I didn't realize that I was hurting someone inside. I'm sorry for making fun of you, Ana."

I could see the hurt showing on Ana's face. She looked at

the floor then at me. "Apology accepted," she mumbled. I gave her a hug for being a person who shows good character.

"Now let's get the class started. We have a lot of information to cover."

After an hour of class, Ms. Flores walked into the room. "Ali, may I speak to you for a moment?"

"Oh sure. Class I'll be right back."

Entering Ms. Flores office, she looked at me. "Close the door, please. Ali, I have just received an email about a competition among all of the schools in our province. It's called Scholastic Studies Competition. It covers math, science, literature, and spelling. It will be broken down into different grade levels and is open to all students who wants to participate. I need to know, do you think our students here would like to take on this challenge?"

Smiling brightly. "When is this supposed to take place? And where?"

'It will be held in Legaspi at the Bicol University on Saturday, February thirteenth. That gives you about four months to prepare."

"I like it. Let's ask the students if they would like to take on this challenge."

Ms. Flores and I stepped up to the front of the classroom while Med was giving a lecture. Seeing us standing there looking at him, he stopped talking so we could tell the class what we just learned.

Ms. Flores looked at her notes, then she raised her head up, "Class. I have received an email pertaining to an academic competition among all of the schools in the province. Ali and I wanted to present it to you to see if you would want to take on this challenge. It covers math, sciences, literature, and spelling. All of the provinces in the country will be taking the same test. The Board of Education in Manila wants to know how the students in our country are doing academically compared to other countries."

Showing excitement in my voice, I had to speak up. "Everyone. I just want to say that a challenge such as this is going to be hard. If you want to take it on, I can stay after school to help anybody who would like the extra teaching. I have taken such a test as this several years back and they word the questions to make you think. You must learn to find the key words of the sentence, then you can find the answer. I'll show you what I mean." Taking a piece of chalk, I put a sentence on the blackboard to a science problem. "Read the sentence and break it down. Find the key word or words and then work the problem."

Chesah knew what I had put on the board was a problem that NASA had to solve. After several minutes had passed, I counted five students who had completed the question.

"Now this kind of question is not what is going to be on all of the grade levels. Each level will have questions that are written for your age group. So, don't let this kind of problem scare you. And, the five students who had raised their hands, please come forward." They seemed a little reluctant at first about standing in front of a group.

"You must conquer any fears that you may have of standing in front of a group of people. This contest will have you working a problem on a board in front of hundreds of people. Can you show me how each one of you came about your answer?"

Each person took turns on how they derived the solution to the problem.

"You are correct. The problem that you solved was one that NASA had to solve on the ISS. Whether it's there in space or here on earth, these kinds of problems must be solved for civilization to grow and move forward. If you can solve problems like this, companies around the world are looking for bright young minds to help them move forward."

After the students returned to their seats, we waited to see who wanted to take on this challenge. Chesah was the first person to raise her hand, then eight more came forward. Out of the thirty-two students, nine wanted to take the challenge.

Juan stood up. "When is this challenge supposed to take place and where?"

I looked at Juan. "February thirteenth at Bicol University in Legaspi City. That gives us approximately four months to prepare for it."

"Juan, are you up for it?"

"I'll have to pass. I'm not any good at math."

"I understand. You would be our star singer if or when such a contest comes about."

He smiled at my complement.

All nine of the students that had raised their hands had a smile on their face. I could hear them talking to each other. "Now, this is my kind of challenge."

A thought came to mind. "They sound a lot like me."

Chesah rolled her chair over towards me. "I like it," she said with excitement in her voice.

"Didn't you take on a challenge a few years back?" she asked.

"I did. I participated in the Battle of the Minds Contest. It went national and international. The finals were held in Tokyo."

"I also heard that you lost it on the last question."

I stayed silent for a moment. "I did. It proves a point that we are all human and we can and will make mistakes. I hope that I don't make the same mistake again." Pulling the nine students away from the rest of the group, "I want you to work on these problems. There are science equations and math. These areas are what most schools tend to hit on the hardest. I will check on your progress in a few minutes. I need to get the others working on an assignment."

"Med, two of the nine students are in your group. I want to push them a little harder in the science and math fields. Are you okay with that?"

"Oh sure. I know that it's going to take a lot of instruction in order to compete in this challenge."

"I know the other schools have had a great head start on teaching. But, we can only try, and it just might make some of the children here be noticed by different families."

Med just smiled at me. "That would be wonderful if some more of the children here were adopted."

"I know that's right," I said.

With everyone busy on working assignments, I didn't see Neala. She tries to blend in so she doesn't stand out. I looked everywhere inside the buildings but had no luck. After about ten minutes, I gave up looking and went back to the classroom.

Seeing her enter, I made my way over to where she was standing. I have looked everywhere for you, "Are you okay.'

She gave me a slight smile. "I'm okay. I just wanted to do some checking of the school buildings. You know security work."

I knew what she was talking about. We don't need another disaster in our lives.

# ~Chapter Twenty-Three~

A re you ready?" Med asked Ms. Flores and Juan as they were entering his SUV. Juan's face had jubilation showing as he shut the rear door. "Juan, you are scheduled to perform at three o'clock." Ms. Flores smiled. She knew that Juan will now have a chance at showing the world what he can do.

"Med, thank you for doing this for Juan and thanks for inviting me along."

"You're welcome. I thought you may like to get away for a little while. We should be in Naga City by ten a.m.."

Looking into my mirror. "Juan, this is just a small gathering that Father Bayon had told me about. He thinks that it would be a good thing for you to perform in. Sort of getting your feet wet kinda thing." I agreed with him. "You start out small and see how things go. If you like it, then we move up the ladder to larger venues."

Ms. Flores looked over the passenger seat. "Are you nervous?"

Juan fiddled with his hands. "Kinda."

Med looked at him in the rear-view mirror. "Do your breathing exercises like I taught you, you'll be okay." Med looked back again in his rear-view mirror. "You should have seen me when I had to do my first surgery. I had practiced the procedure in school, and I was good at it. But when I had to perform the surgery on a live human being, well, I had the nervous shakes something terrible."

"How did it go on your first time?" Juan asked.

"I made it through the procedure okay and the patient is still alive today. Afterwards, I knelt down right there next to the patients bed and thanked our Lord for his guidance."

Ms. Flores patted Med's arm, "You're a good man Montoya."

"Thanks for the complement, Ms. Flores."

"My name is Josie. Josie Flores."

"Thanks again. I was beginning to wonder if you had a first name." She smiled back.

Pulling into the parking lot of the Naga City Hope Christian High School, we had a time trying to find a parking space. Having to circle the block several times, we parked three blocks away from the school. Once we entered the building, Juan found the sign-in table.

"Mr. Gonzales, you are scheduled for three p.m. Good luck."

Juan looked up "Thanks."

I looked at Josie and Juan. "Are you hungry? We have almost three hours before show time." They agreed. We left to find something to eat and came across a Chinese restaurant on the outskirts of town where we filled up with their delicious food.

Juan glanced at us. "I'm stuffed. Hope I can still walk."

We laughed at his demeanor.

Josie looked at me. "Let's go back. I want to see how the other contestants are doing."

Returning to the same parking space, we made our way into the auditorium. Finding seats, we listened to the students singing their hearts out.

At a few minutes before three, Juan made his way to the stage.

"I hope he doesn't freeze up."

Josie spoke. "He'll do fine." Juan's name was called. We watched as he knelt down for a moment. He was saying a prayer. We knew that no matter what happens, he would be okay. Holding the microphone, he was silent for several seconds, then he began to sing his version of 'Halleluiah.' Afterwards the whole place was cheering and clapping for this shy young man. Juan left the stage returning to us. We both patted him on his back and congratulated him on his performance.

After the last contestant had performed, we sat anxiously waiting to hear the winners. After another forty-minute wait, the MC returned to the stage. "As everyone is well aware, choosing a winner among the more than fifty contestants was difficult to say the least, but we must choose a winner for this competition. And our third place goes to Maria Rosa. Our second-place winner is Juan Gonzales. And our first-place winner goes to our very own Mika De Leon."

Juan returned to the stage to receive his award. Making his way to where we stood, a man approached him. The three of us listened as he began his speech.

"My name is Miguel Andrada. I'm a talent scout for the Philippine National Choir. I was impressed with the way you sing. I'm looking for candidates to join our organization." He paused for several seconds to let the information sink in. "Here is my card. If you would like to try out for our group, give me a call sometime." He turned away and left.

Josie and Med looked at each other then at Juan. His voice sounded a little choked up. "That was interesting, wasn't it? I have never seen a talent scout before. And now one has approached me to try out for a famous choir."

Juan looked at the card he held in his hands then slowly raised his head. "Maybe one day, I might be ready to take on the world."

Med smiled. "You know Juan, no matter how this outcome

works out, you're still a winner. I think your world is about to take you to the next level of your life."

\*\*\*\*\*

Arriving at the children's home bright and early on a Monday morning, Neala, Chesah and I could hear a piano being played. Seeing Med's SUV already in the parking lot, I had an idea of whom was playing the music.

"Do you want to check out to see who's playing?" I asked Chesah.

"Sure," she said and rolled herself towards the music door. Cracking the door to just a small opening, we could see Ana and Med sitting on the piano bench.

Med turned in his seat when he heard the door open.

With a joyful voice, "I thought it may be you and Ana. She's playing very well."

Med smiled at my compliment. "She's performing much better than before."

Ana looked at me with a smile as big as she could put on her face.

"You go girl. It won't be too long before you will rock this house." I walked over to her and gave her a high-five.

Chesah didn't want to be left out. She pushed her chair next to her. "Can I have some of that?" Ana gave her a high-five as well.

"Oh yeah. Now that's what I'm talking about." Turning her chair around, she wheeled herself back towards the classroom. Neala and I left closing the door.

Returning to the classroom, I found Ms. Flores standing in front of the room. As soon as everyone was seated, she began to speak.

"This past Saturday, Juan, Med and I went to a christian

singing competition in Naga City. Juan performed in front of more than one-hundred people and did very well for himself. Though he came in second place, he is a winner to us and to this school. He had to overcome his shyness and sang his heart out. We could not be prouder of him. Also, I might add that he was approached by a talent scout looking for a person to perform with the Philippine National Choir. Not too bad for a young man from the Albay Children's Home."

Everyone began to congratulate him on his achievement. Juan stood up. "Thanks. This means a lot to me."

I strolled over to him and shook his hand. "Well done. You are on the right path. I'm very proud to know you."

Juan looked at my face. "Thanks for believing in me."

"You're welcome."

Ms. Flores left the room, and we began our day of teaching. Watching over the class, some of the older students were helping the younger kids with their work. I made my way around the room looking at what each student was working on. I found the preschoolers laying on the floor coloring different things in their workbooks. I got down on the floor with them. Picking up a crayon, the three-year-old boy saw what I was looking at on a workbook.

"You have the wrong color for that giraffe." I looked over at him. "I sure do. What color should it be?" I asked.

"They have yellow stripes and brown patches on them. He looked into the basket of crayons. These would be best for it."

"Thank you for your insight. I was about to make a mistake." I stayed for several minutes coloring the giraffe, then I gave it to the young boy. You can have it," I said smiling at him.

He smiled back and thanked me for the picture.

Working with other preschoolers on their pictures, I felt alive being with them. I knew that this was what our Lord wanted me to do with my life, to help others and teach them to be proud of their accomplishments in life. I got up on my knees. Bowing my head, I said a prayer. "Lord, the wonderful gift that you gave me, I will give it back to the people many times over."

Juan knelt down next to me. "May I join you?"

"If you would like too," I said.

I looked up at the others in the room. They were in awe watching me.

"I will tell you about my life. You need to know who I am and why I'm here. I have no secrets to keep from you."

A senior girl asked. "Why are you telling us now? Why this moment instead of when you first met us."

"I had a feeling come over me just a few minutes ago. I don't know where or when they do show up, but I get them a lot. I don't know exactly how to explain it, but I know that our Lord has something to do with it."

"You can talk to our Lord?" she asked.

"No. But he knows what we are thinking. I wish I could explain it better than what I'm trying to say. Most of you know that I was given the gift of knowledge by our Lord. I have been using my gift to help others. I have invented a product that makes concrete stronger so a building can stand up to a super typhoon and not collapse. Now I'm using my gift to teach others so they too can go out in this world to better themselves or help the people in their communities. That's why I'm grateful for my precious gift that our Lord gave me. To help others anyway I can. Now you know why I like to say a prayer thanking him."

I noticed the room was quiet. "I didn't mean to stop everyone from working on their projects. I apologize for the interruptions."

Ms. Flores looked at me. "No apologies necessary. Sometimes we can all use a little boosting up of our spirit."

There was a knock on our classroom door. Med opened it to find Father Bayon standing on the front porch. I sprang over to where he was standing. Taking his right hand and putting it to my forehead, all the other children saw me and did the same.

He seemed surprised at the reception that he was receiving. "Did I miss something?" he asked.

"I kinda stopped the class for a moment and said a prayer." Then I explained why I did.

"I see," he replied.

"Class, your teacher is not a normal human being by any sense of the word. She has been blessed by our Lord and you have among you the greatest teacher to ever live in our country. Someday when you grow up, you will understand all of the knowledge you carry with you. And I also think that Dr. Montoya is one of the greatest surgeons that lives among us. His knowledge has saved countless lives over the years."

A fourteen-year-old boy spoke up. "If Ali and Dr. Montoya are so great at teaching, why are they here and not at some university."

I couldn't sit back and listen without making a statement. "I am here because Father Bayon asked me to come by and see the students here. I have been to several universities who wanted me to teach, but when the faculty found out that I will be teaching there, they all wanted to quit. Most of you know how it feels to be rejected. It hurts deep inside to not be wanted and cast out because of who you are. I too have been rejected more than once because of my gift. Society does not like someone who is different. When I saw you for the first time, I knew that this is the place that I needed to be. With others like me who have been rejected for just being born. These are harsh words, but I know I speak the truth." Everyone who was old enough, knew what I was saying.

Father Bayon got up from his chair. "What Ali is saying is true. We all must find out who we are and what are we going to do with our life. Ali has discovered that she belongs here. So, learn from her and you will be forever grateful for the knowledge that you have gained."

Picking up his possessions, he faced the group. "I must go now and check on the people at the hospital."

"Goodbye, Father," I said as he closed the door.

# ~Chapter Twenty-Four~

Working with a vengeance, Med and I had the seven students who were going to compete and hitting the books hard. With Christmas almost upon us, we only had a short time of pushing them to the limits of their knowledge. One day after the main class was over, I stopped everyone from what they were doing.

"I just want to know if this group thinks that I'm pushing you too hard. You guys have been working so diligently to take yourselves to the next level."

Everyone looked at each other, then at me. Med made his way over to where we were having our conversation.

The oldest boy of the group stood up. "We like the way you two are teaching us. Nobody has ever taken the time to help us like you two are doing. And for that, we are all grateful for your help." They all agreed.

"Thanks," I said.

Med looked at me then at everyone sitting in front of us. "I'm very proud of each of you for wanting to better yourselves. It means a lot to me to see you work so hard at pushing yourselves above the others. Your future holds many opportunities."

A girl of about fifteen stood up from her chair. "We don't know how we are going to continue our education after we leave here. We cannot afford to go to college."

I looked into Med's eyes. I saw a twinkle of light shining

from them.

The Saturday before Christmas, I asked Ms. Flores and Med if we could have a small party for the kids here at the children's home. Ms. Flores and Med liked the idea.

I became excited. "We can have a meal catered in and have the children hang their parol (a colorful star shaped lantern), then we can go to the evening mass. We might be able to get Juan to sing for us at the mass. That is if he would like to do it."

Med spoke up. "I'll ask Father Bayon first. If he says it's okay, then I'll ask Juan."

"That would be wonderful," I said with jubilation in my voice.

I made some calls about having the food catered. With Christmas Day falling on a Wednesday this year, I planned to have this party on a Monday evening.

Med had received word from Father Bayon that it would be wonderful if Juan would sing with the choir on Christmas Eve.

"Okay, that's great news. Now, we just need to ask Juan."

Ms. Flores spoke up. "Check the music room. That's where I normally find him when he's not studying."

Med left to check. Opening the door to just a small opening, he found Juan and Ana sitting at the piano. He listened to Ana play and Juan practicing his notes. Opening the door at a snail's pace, Med made his way into the room.

"Juan, I have something to ask of you."

"What do you need?" he asked.

"Father Bayon has asked if you would like to perform with the churches choir Tuesday evening for Christmas Eve Mass?"

Juan sat quiet for several seconds. "I would like that."

"Great. Let's call Father Bayon so you both can put something together". After dialing the Father, Juan made arrangements to meet with the choir and Father Bayon.

Med was full of joy. "That's wonderful. And also Ms.

Flores, Ali, and I are putting on a small party here for Monday evening. We will be having the food catered in from a very nice restaurant."

Juan and Ana smiled. "That sounds fantastic," Juan replied. "We'll leave you two alone so you can return to your practicing"

Shutting the door, Med and I returned to the classroom. Finding Neala sitting off in a corner watching something on her phone, I approached her.

"Neala, can you find a caterer who can deliver food for about fifty people for Monday evening? We are going to have a small party for the students here at the children's home."

Neala stopped what she was doing and looked up at me. "I'll check and get back to you in a few minutes."

"Thanks," I said returning to the class.

"Hey everyone. We are going to have a small Christmas party here Monday evening. I have Neala checking into finding us a caterer to provide food for the party. We should know something in a little while. Would you please tell everyone about this party? Ms. Flores, Med and I thought it would be nice to share an evening with some great food and friendship. In the meantime, let's return to what we were working on."

Med and I kept everyone busy working on math and science problems. I even through in some spelling words that seem to cause a lot of concern to a lot of students.

I kept up this pace until almost five p.m.

"Okay everyone. Tomorrow is Sunday. I think you guys need a day off from so much studying. Let's stop for today and we'll start again Monday morning."

Neala strolled over to where I was standing. "I have found a caterer who says they can work with us. I told them to bring Pancit, (a yellow-colored noodle dish with pork, egg, and shrimp), Christmas ham, Spaghetti (Filipino style), Puto Bumbong (purple rice cake), and Leche Flan (Filipino style baked custard of creme caramel).”

"Sounds wonderful. I'll let the group know what to expect.”

*****

Arriving home with Chesah and Dalisay, I told our parents and Minda about the party that we are having on Monday evening.

Minda looked up at me. "Are we invited to your party?”

"Why of course. I'm hoping that you, mom and dad will attend. We're having food catered in. It's just a small gathering of family and friends.”

*****

Sunday morning after mass, I found Father Bayon speaking with Juan. I strolled over to where they were talking.

"Father, can you come to our small party we are having tomorrow evening at the children's home? We are having food catered in and maybe we can sing some Christmas songs.”

"I would love to join you," Father Bayon said.

"What time?”

"Say around six-thirty?”

"I'll be there," he said smiling.

I turned and left Juan and the Father discussing the Christmas Eve Mass.

*****

Monday morning was a flurry of activity. Ms. Flores had everyone working on cleaning the floors, dusting, and just doing a general cleaning of our classroom. The children's home dining room was just too small to handle approximately fifty people.

Ms. Flores saw me walking in. She said. "I'm having the

children do a general cleaning of the room for our party tonight." Chesah and Dalisay saw their friends doing their chores and they wanted to pitch in. The only people I didn't see was Med, Juan and Ana."

I was looking in the direction of children singing, and Ms. Flores stated, "They're all in the music room. I think they may have a surprise for us tonight."

"Oh wonderful," I said with a joyful voice.

Returning to the classroom, the remainder of kids had the room spotless.

"Hey everyone, we will work on our assignments until three o'clock. Then we can bring in some tables for the caterers to set the food on while we hang the parols. The food should be here about six p.m." Everything was going as planned.

The caterers made it just before six p.m. and began to setup our feast. Father Bayon arrived at six-twenty.

"Good evening, Father," I said, taking his right hand and putting it against my forehead.

"Good evening, Ali. This is a wonderful idea that you and Med came up with. I don't think the children's home has ever had a Christmas meal catered in before."

"Thank you, Father. It was the least we could do for the children."

He smiled putting his hand on my head. "You're a wonderful person Ali Cruz. Our Lord knew what he was doing when he gave you your gift. You have touched the hearts of so many."

The Father left me and headed over to where several children were setting up things or hanging their parols. I watched the smiles show up on their faces as the Father talked to them.

Hearing my name being called, I noticed Minda, and my parents had arrived. With Dalisay hanging onto my and Minda's finger, Chesah moved her chair in front of us saying, "Make way, make way."

I caught the look on Minda's face as most of the kids wanted to ask her questions about how she graduated from college at such an early age. Minda's face was lit up with excitement.

She told her story about her life and how she tried out for the Battle of the Minds contest, a few years back. The class was mesmerized listening to her speak. Chesah saw the look on my face as I listened to Minda.

"You had something to do with Minda and her education. Listening to her, I can see part of you."

I smiled at her. "All I did was guide her. She earned everything by herself. She wanted a better life and to be somebody in this world."

Chesah smiled at me. "You did a wonderful job by helping her. Maybe one day you can guide me."

"I would like that," I said as I gave her a hug.

Without notice we heard noises coming from the hallway. The piano was being rolled into the classroom by a group of boys.

"I think we're going to have a show for tonight." Chesah smiled. "I think you are right."

Ms. Flores rang a small bell. "Would everyone find a chair to stand next to." After the commotion of bodies moving about, the room fell silent. Father Bayon stood next to Ms. Flores.

"I would like to say a prayer. Please bow your heads."

After the prayer, Ms. Flores asked everyone to be seated. "For this evenings gathering, I would like to say thanks to Med and Ali for putting together this wonderful festival for us. They have touched the hearts of so many."

The group started cheering when Ms. Flores silenced the group. "We have a special treat after we eat for this evening. Juan and Ana are going to perform for us." The group started cheering again.

"Now if you would like to make your way to the buffet line

and help yourself to this wonderful food."

After everyone was seated again, Ana and Juan headed over to the piano.

Ms. Flores stood up. "Everyone, I would like to present Ana and Juan. They are going to sing a few Christmas songs for us. Please give them a round of applause." Everybody began clapping or whistling. Then the room went quiet.

Ana began to play. She gave it everything she had. Even though she hit a few wrong notes, she and Juan's performance were wonderful.

After they had finished, Ana and Juan stood in front of the crowd. I noticed the tears in Ana's eyes. She was happy at her performance. Juan gave her a hug as they returned to their seats.

Med stood up. "I have an announcement to make. I have decided to give any person here a chance to go to college. Everything will be paid for. That is if you want to go. Some of you may want to go to a trade school. Which is also a great choice to make. I will do the same for you as well."

Everybody stood up and began cheering. Several of the older kids had a look of astonishment on their faces.

A girl of about fifteen replied. "You would do that for me?"

Med replied. "I would. And for all of you, if you choose to go."

I felt a warm feeling in my heart. Med is the kindest most unselfish person that I know.

The look on Ms. Flores face was priceless. In all of her years, she has never met two people like Med and I. Someone who cares so much for the children of this home.

Father Bayon raised his hands to his shoulder height. "May I say something?" The room fell silent. "I would like to give thanks to Ali and Med for their generosity. For this wonderful meal and for helping the children here now and for their future. I want to also give thanks to Ana and Juan for providing us with their Christmas music. For this is a joyful time in our lives. I would also like to say a prayer to our Lord for his guidance in bringing this all together."

As the party began to wind down, I looked at Med. "I don't know about next year, but this one will go down into the history books about this home as the best that has ever happened here."

Med sat back in his chair. "I know that's right."

My parents, Minda, Chesah and Dalisay stood next to us. Med stood up as my father reached out to give him a handshake and then a hug. Standing back, he said. "You two have touched the hearts of so many. This day will always be remembered." I looked at Minda. She too had tears in her eyes. The three of us stood around Chesah's chair.

Minda commented to Chesah. "I told you the Cruz family knows how to throw a one-two punch. We don't hold nothing back."

Chesah looked up at me. "You sure do," was all she said smiling.

Christmas Eve Mass will be a day that no one in our community will ever forget. After the sermon from Father Bayon, Juan and the church choir performed their Christmas music. The looks on everyone's face expressed how much they were enjoying the moment. Afterwards, we thanked Father Bayon and Juan for this wonderful blessing.

*****

Christmas Day, the Cruz family awoke to the smells of fresh coffee and some hot coco for Dalisay. It seems our parents were in a happy mood. After us four girls made our way into our living room, the smells of cooked breakfast permeated our senses.

We had eggs, rice, sweet sausage, and coffee.

After our breakfast, the four of us girls were watching the

Christmas shows on the television when our parents made their way towards us. Our parents handed each of us a gift. The look of surprise on both Chesah and Dalisay's face was priceless. Either one has ever received a personal gift before. Just when they were about to open their presents, I heard a knock on our front door.

"Who is it?" I asked.

"Neala."

Opening the door to my dearest friend, "Please come in. Chesah and Dalisay are about to open their gifts."

"Any coffee made?"

"It sure is," I said as I left to get Neala a cup.

The five of us stood around watching Dalisay begin to open her present. Her eyes widened when she saw a small laptop.

"A laptop for me." Then the tears formed in her eyes.

"I love it," she wailed as she opened the top cover.

Our father looked at her. "You need to have one of your sisters help you with it. They will teach you how to use it. Your mom and I didn't want you to be left out on the intelligence department. This will give you a good start on it anyway."

"Thanks mom, dad. It's beautiful."

Chesah started to open her gift. She too received a laptop. But hers was a top-of-the-line model.

"Mom and dad asked me what you needed. I told them a laptop. You will be getting calls and emails from the PAGSAS Office. They seem very interested in you. This way you can learn more about your future and what you can look forward to if that is the direction you want to proceed."

Neala opened her bag. And this is from Minda, Ali, and me. We know that you will be needing it to receive calls." Chesah took the small box from Neala. Inside was a smart phone.

"Oh my. I never dreamed of something like this ever happening to me."

I stared into Chesah's eyes. "Don't get caught with your

phone at the children's home. Keep it turned off while you are there. Ms. Flores does not want any of the kids to have one. We wanted you to be ready in case you are called upon or you have an emergency and need to reach one of us. All of our phone numbers have already been programed into it."

Little Dalisay picked up my hand. "And for you," I said. Neala reached into her bag again and brought out a small package. Handing it over to her, she began to tear the wrapping paper off. Inside was a small cross on a gold chain.

"It's beautiful," she said holding it up so everyone could get a look at it.

"May I?" Minda said as she took the cross from Dalisay.

She put it around her neck and hooked the clasp.

Chesah took a picture with her new phone of Dalisay with her new laptop and gold cross. I did the same of Chesah and her laptop and phone.

Our parents then handed Minda and I each an envelope. Inside was some cash.

Thanks mom and dad for these wonderful Christmas presents. Each one of us gave them a hug. Then we all said aloud "Merry Christmas."

# ~Chapter Twenty-Five~

With the school's competition just one week away, I kept a vigorous pace of putting more knowledge into the competing student heads. They all knew that they were going head-to-head with some very intelligent people. Med would sometimes take over the class, giving them medical questions, biology and science questions that were pertinent in the medical field. I knew that we had to cover as much as possible. This challenge will be difficult to pass, but an endeavor that they will never forget.

Saturday, February thirteenth, Med hired a local tour bus to bring everyone from the children's home to watch the top students compete against the best students in the province. As we made our way towards Bicol University in Legaspi City where the contest was being held, the bus came alive as we sang familiar songs. I was enjoying the camaraderie part of this group. I felt alive like I have never felt before. As soon as we arrived, Ms. Flores, Med and I left the group to find the sign-in table. After receiving the name tags for the competitors, we found a place for our group to sit. Chesah rolled her chair into the aisle next to me, and Dalisay and Neala sat on the opposite side. The fifty or so students were called up to the front rows of tables.

The announcer began to make her speech. "Each of you have a number that has been assigned to you. Your number is on the back of the chair and on the table. When I call your name, come and pick up your packet and find your seat number. As soon as everyone is ready, we will begin this contest." I noticed that they had a smaller table for the students who were in wheelchairs. Chesah sat there with a boy from another school.

"Now that you have your packet, you have two hours to finish. If you finish early, raise your hand and a monitor will pick it up. Do not talk to anyone and leave the room."

"Any questions? You may open you packet and begin."

Crossing my fingers, Dalisay saw me and did the same. She looked up at me and smiled. I picked up her small hand. While sitting there watching others take this test, time just seemed to drag by. But I knew how the students mind was wanting more time to answer the questions. Two hours was just not enough time to finish.

The announcer walked onto the stage. Standing in front of the microphone she clicked the on-button. "Time is up. Please put your pencils down. Hand your packet to the monitors and exit this room. Do not talk to anyone as you leave. Out in the hallway, you will find the restrooms on the right side of this building and we have provided you with some refreshments on the left. Your test will be graded, and you may return in an hour."

Med and I left with our competitors. I wanted to know what this test was like. *What did the questions cover? Subject matter, how many, etc.* As soon as we had our group gathered, I wanted to know if the material that Med and I had covered pertained to the questions.

They all agreed, it did.

"I know that I pushed you guys hard, but I knew that we didn't have much time to cover these subjects. You have to remember that the rest of these students have been studying this information for a lot longer than you have. No matter the outcome, you are all winners. We are proud of you taking on the entire school system. When you are finished with your refreshments, we'll head back into the room with the others."

Everyone had just returned when the announcer made her way on stage.

"The grading of these test has now been completed. I will be calling out only three names from the elementary grade level, then the high school level. Starting with the third-place finisher. When I call your name, please come on stage, state you name and what school you attend."

The third place in the elementary level went to a boy from Legaspi City. The second place went to a girl from Sorsogon, and the first place went to our very own Rolado Ramos.

Rolado walked onto the stage doing his kinda I'm cool walk. Everyone in our group started whistling and clapping. Rolado raise his metal above his head as he exited the stage.

After they received their awards, the high school kids were up next. The third place goes to a boy from Naga City Science High School. The second place goes to a girl from Legaspi City Science High School. And the first-place winner is Chesah Torres from the Albay Children's Home.

Chesah began yelling "I won, I won."

With excitement in my voice, I yelled, "Alright, way to go. Now go and receive you award." I had a massive, large smile on my face. Since she couldn't roll her chair onto the stage, the announcer made her way over to Chesah. Standing next to Chesah's chair, she presented her with a first-place metal.

I noticed the tears in her eyes. With a sobbing voice. "My name is Chesah Torres. And I'm from the Albay Children's Home. My teachers are Dr. Med Montoya and Ali Cruz. I could not have made it this far if it wasn't for the teachings from these two wonderful people. And for that, I will always be grateful." The whole room stood up to congratulate Chesah. She sat there holding her prize up as people began taking photos of her.

After the excitement had died down, Chesah returned to our

group. Everybody congratulated her on winning this prestigious award. I gave her a big hug. "You earned this."

Chesah smiled at me. "Thanks Ali, thanks for everything."

"You're welcome."

Our group was making our way out of the building when a man from the Albay School District Office approached me.

"Ms. Cruz, may I have a word with you?"

"Sure," I said.

"I have been following your history on teaching for some time now. Would you like to teach at a university? I can guarantee you any position that you would like."

"Thanks for the offer, but I have already been asked this same question before. When the teaching faculty learned that I would be teaching with them, they all threatened to quit. I have found my place in this world, a place that makes me feel wanted."

"It's too bad that society is driving away the best teachers to ever walk this planet. Your knowledge would put any school at the top of the list. Students would come from around the world to be taught by a teacher such as yourself. If you ever change your mind, give me a call. Here is my card."

"Thanks," I said taking his card.

Sitting in the bus on our way home, I kept fumbling the card I held in my hands. Ms. Flores watched me as I kept flipping it back and forth. "Anything important?" she asked.

"I was offered a teaching job at any university that I liked."

"What did you tell them?"

"I already had a job. And I'm happy to have it."

Ms. Flores smiled at me. "What you and Med have done with the children here will make their lives prosperous. They will never forget how you came into their world and gave them hope for a better life."

As soon as our tour bus pulled up to the front of the children's home, we were greeted by a large group of people.

Ms. Flores was not expecting to have an audience waiting for us.

"What's up?" she asked.

"I called Father Bayon and told him about our trip. He must have spread the word around town."

The look on Ms. Flores face seemed shocked. "I see," as we were beginning to exit the bus. I noticed the mayor and several school administrators were watching us as well as a camera crew from a television station in Legaspi City.

A news reporter approached Ms. Flores.

"Any comments on how the children did in this academic competition?"

"Our children here did well in this competition. They scored a first in elementary level and a first in the high school level."

"Who are their teachers?" the news woman asked.

"They are Ms. Ali Cruz and Dr. Med Montoya."

"Did I hear you right? You have Ms. Ali Cruz teaching here?"

"We do. Father Bayon introduced Ali to us, and she asked if she could teach here. She was approved by the Board of Directors and has been here for about five months."

"So, you're saying that it only took her about five months to teach the kids here, to this degree of high intelligence."

"Well, kinda, I guess. We already have several very intelligent kids that live here. Ali and Dr. Montoya just brought out their hidden talents. Now for the first time in their lives, they can see a real future for themselves."

The news woman shoved the microphone towards me.
"Ms. Cruz, what are your thoughts on how this competition went?"

"Every student that participated deserves to be noticed. They all worked extra hard for this contest. And for that I'm proud to know them. As for Rolado and Chesah, they deserved to win. The competition from all of the different schools in our province was outstanding."

"So, are you taking some or all the credit for their achievement?"

"No, not at all. They did all of the work. All Med and I did was guide them. They earned the right to their win. And we could not be more proud of them."

After a few more questions were asked from the mayor and the school administrators, the news team had their story for the evening news.

Neala looked at me. "That went well."

"Yeah, about as good as it's going to be since this is not an official public or private school."

Father Bayon stepped over to where Neala and I were standing.

"Ali, I'm so blessed to know you. I know deep down in my heart that our Lord picked the right person."

"Father, may we say a prayer?"

"I do believe our Lord would like that." Chesah rolled her chair next to me and Dalisay held my right hand. Father Bayon raised his voice so he could be heard over those talking. "Everyone, I would like to say a prayer for this group." Everybody began to gather around us. As we were bowing our heads, Chesah reached over and took my left hand. She then squeezed it. I looked at her and she tilted her head and moved her eyes upwards. I looked at what she was trying to say to me. Med was holding Ms. Flores's hand. I looked back at Chesah. She whispered. "Our Lord works in mysterious ways."

Tilting my head upwards so that I could look at the heaven, I whispered back. "He sure does."

We were beginning to say our prayer to our Lord when we noticed the lights flashing from a patrol car. All of us turned our attention to see what was going on when two police officers made their way towards us. I locked my eyes on the officer carrying what seem to be a small child in his arms.

Ms. Flores rushed over to where they were standing. "What's going on?" she asked the officers.

"We found this little boy on the street a couple of nights ago. We have not been able to find his parents, and nobody has stepped up to claim him. We took him to the hospital to have him checked out to make sure that he was okay. We have been instructed to bring him here."

"I see," Ms. Flores replied. "I'll take him." As the officer handed over this beautiful little boy, he began to cry. All I could hear was "Momma. I want my momma." I felt my hands being squeezed by Chesah and Dalisay. Looking at their faces, they both had tears running down their cheeks. This little boy had just entered into our world. A place where you will always feel abandoned.

# ~THE END~

*"Traveling to another part of the world opened up a passion with photography. Photographing people in another culture and in which they live was not only intriguing, but it led me to the inspiration of writing, such as my first book, "Miracles Are Chosen. "*

## Michael J. Alsup

**About the author**:
*Place: Torrence, California*
*Currently resides in Beaumont TX*

**Memberships:**
*Beaumont Camera Club*
*Texas Gulf Coast Writers Group*
*Philippine Association of Beaumont TX*

**MICHAEL J. ALSUP**

**NEXT UPCOMING BOOK:**

**Coming Early Fall**

# LOST ROADS BACK

Sam Withers ran his fingers along the edge of the pages of his grandfather's weathered book. After a discovery of a treasure map, Sam learns about a lost treasure that has been missing for more than one hundred and fifty years. Working with some of the kids from school, they begin to search for the treasure. Awakened by the sound of gunfire, Sam is mesmerized as he watched men face their inevitable deaths as they marched towards each other. Survival during this dangerous time in history, is top priority. Sam is now forced to deal with bandits, the local law enforcement, and a pretty doctor's daughter. His life will never be the same.

With family and friends gathered around his hospital bed, plans are made to finish what they had started. To continue the journey to find the answers that has plagued Sam's grandfather for so long.

Next book in the

*Ali Cruz Series:*

~

# When Love Touches
# The Heart

**Coming soon
2023**